Walking down the steps, ~~Jo~~ ~~her~~ car was parked behind his own: a white ~~Mercedes~~. He guessed that it was Voss's car and started for it, expecting the man would step from it to greet him.

Jon was right about one thing: Voss was behind the wheel. But he did not step out. Instead, his head was tilted awkwardly against the headrest. The seat belt had been removed. The man's eyes and mouth were open. There was a deep wound in the center of his throat from which great amounts of blood had poured. The white shirt Voss had worn had been ripped open, exposing the man's chest.

Starting just below the wound and running downward to his abdomen were three long scars.

"...'very good and very timely' with strong local color."

—*Booknews*, The Poisoned Pen

Previously published Worldwide Mystery titles by
RAY SIPHERD

DANCE OF THE SCARECROWS
THE AUDUBON QUARTET

RAY SIPHERD

THE DEVIL'S HAWK

W💣RLDWIDE.

TORONTO • NEW YORK • LONDON
AMSTERDAM • PARIS • SYDNEY • HAMBURG
STOCKHOLM • ATHENS • TOKYO • MILAN
MADRID • WARSAW • BUDAPEST • AUCKLAND

For my Father and the memory of my Mother

THE DEVIL'S HAWK

A Worldwide Mystery/January 2004

First published by St. Martin's Press LLC.

ISBN 0-373-26480-1

Printed in U.S.A.

Acknowledgments

With Special Thanks to

Kevin Dahl, former Executive Director of the Tucson Audubon Society, for his expertise in everything from the ornithological to the typographical; Suzette M. Davis, for her splendid research; Bonnie Grande, for her fluency in Spanish, which was far greater than mine; Rob Daniels, former Public Relations Officer, United States Border Patrol, Tucson Sector, for providing fascinating details of Border Patrol operations; my agents, Michael V. Carlisle and Michelle Tessler, for their enthusiasm and encouragement; my editors at St. Martin's Press, Carin Siegfried and Tom Dunne, for their guidance and keen judgment; and always, for more reasons than I can say, my wife, Anne Marie.

Downward to darkness, on extended wings.
                    —Wallace Stevens
                       "Sunday Morning"

PROLOGUE

THE DOVE BLINKED, mildly curious at their presence, and returned to pecking at a low branch of the mesquite tree.

"Tell me the name of that bird," the mother asked.

"*¡Paloma!*" shouted the boy.

"Speak English. *Inglés*," said the mother. "We are in America now."

The boy thought. He shook his head.

"Dove!" the girl cried. She was eight, two years older than her brother, and knew the names of many birds.

They had played the game at dawn, just as the three had played it in their village in the mountains to the south. Today the mother hoped the game would keep them from asking for more food. When the game ended, they asked anyway, so the mother gave them the last of the fried pork rinds she had brought. But the rinds made them thirsty, and there was little water left to share.

Still, the mother poured a small amount into the children's cupped hands, giving it first to the girl and then to the boy. In his eagerness to drink, he spilled some on her white dress. She was about to scold him but did not. The dress was cotton; it would dry quickly in the heat. And soon they would have all the water they could want.

There were six of them: the mother and the father and their children, and the father's cousin and her son, who was thirteen. They had been led across the border after midnight. Once in Arizona, the smugglers had told them, they would be transported to a house in Tucson. Those who were expecting them would be informed.

The fence that marked the border was of steel chain links. But it had been cut through and tunneled under many times, so that it did not slow the crossing. The smugglers had crossed first, followed by the woman and the teenage boy, and, finally, the mother and father and their children. The adults carried satchels. In them were small plastic bottles filled with water, a package of marshmallows for the children, a jar containing pork rinds, and a few articles of clothing. After walking for a distance, a battered pickup truck approached them. Two men climbed down from the cab of the truck and came to them. The men ordered the six into the back of the truck. The children had been lifted up, the rest climbed aboard, and they drove into the desert night.

Soon the pickup stopped at the bottom of a dry arroyo. The two men in the front climbed out again and came to them. The passenger, who was called *El Cantante*, The Singer, was the first to speak. He told them to come down from the back of the truck and stand in a line facing him. Then he demanded the money they were carrying.

The adults insisted they had none. But when *El Cantante* showed a gun, the father fumbled in his pockets and produced some pesos. The man took them and threw them on the ground. He waved the gun and told the father to remove his shoes. The father did so. The man picked up the shoes, thrust his fingers into them, and withdrew several hundred-dollar bills in U.S. currency.

Now he demanded something more. He stepped forward to the mother. Fondling her long, dark hair, he said something only she could hear. In response, she bowed her head and whispered, *"No, no—por favor."*

Seeing his wife begin to cry, the father became angry with *El Cantante* and shouted. The man said nothing. Instead, he hit the father on the face so hard the father fell to the ground.

The children, too, began to cry at the blood covering their father's face. The driver spoke quickly to *El Cantante*. He nodded. Without looking back, the two got into the pickup truck and drove away.

The mother comforted the children until their crying stopped. Then she tore some fabric from inside the hem of her dress, wet it with water from a plastic bottle, and cleaned the blood from her husband's face.

It was well after midnight. Having no idea where they were and seeing no lights, the six of them slept in the arroyo. The mother and father unrolled a rough mat they had brought for the children. Then, like the cousin and her son, they lay down on the sand, using their satchels as pillows for their heads.

Throughout the night they woke at every sound, fearful of a rattlesnake or scorpion. Although it was June, the coolness surprised them, and they shivered in their thin clothing and drew their arms against themselves for warmth. At dawn, the father made a fire and the six sat close around it.

Then they waited.

The sun rose quickly over the mountains to the east; at first, a shimmering white coin in the sky, bursting suddenly into a fierce brilliance that consumed the sky itself.

And still they waited. But no one came.

So they began to walk. How long they walked, they did not know. Sometimes if the land rose, they would stop and study the horizon for some sign of life—a road, a house, a line of wires leading anywhere. But all they saw was empty desert blanched white by the relentless sun.

At noon they stopped again. Before they had left Mexico they had filled three plastic bottles with water. By now the contents of two had been consumed. In the last bottle, less than a cup remained. It was shared among them. The father kept the empty bottle, hoping they might find a spring from which they could refill it. But they never did.

It was the cousin who began to stumble first. Weak and dizzy from the heat, she slipped and fell against a fishhook cactus. For long moments she sat crying and attempting to remove the sharp barbs from her leg.

The rest waited, offering to help her if they could. She said her son would wait with her and told the others to go on. Soon they would join them. Reluctantly, the man agreed.

The father, the mother, and the children came upon the mission in midafternoon. It was no more than a ruin, actually: one wall with an opening in the center that had been the entrance to the church and pieces of adobe brick suggesting where the other walls had stood. The mission had been built more than three centuries ago, when Spanish Jesuits had sought with limited success to bring Christ's word to the pagan Indians. Yet time, the desert winds, and wars between the Indians and settlers had caused those words to dwindle to a whisper, leaving nothing but the silence that engulfed them now.

The mother stopped before the opening and looked up at the lintel stone above. Carved into it was a small cross.

"Iglesia," she said softly to herself.

She moved through the opening and stopped again. To her left, a piece of rounded stone protruded from the wall. It had served as a receptacle for holy water for those entering the church. Instinctively, the mother placed her fingers into the dry, concave surface of the stone and blessed herself. Then she fell to her knees.

When she did not rise, her husband came to her, kneeling down beside her to give comfort.

"Rest here with the children," he said to her in Spanish. "I will find help."

He stood again, and, putting his hands under her

arms, he dragged her to a section of the wall beside the opening where there was shade, and placed her back against the stones.

"Mamá," the boy said, coming to her and sitting at her right.

The girl also came and sat down at her mother's left. Slowly the mother put her arms around the children. Then she closed her eyes.

When she awoke, the children were still pressed against her, but their skin felt hot and dry. How long had they been there? she asked herself. A week? A month? Was that the Virgin Mary standing at the altar, beckoning?

Now they were in their village in the mountains. She was fetching water from the stream. *"¡Agua! ¡Agua!"* cried the boy and the girl. The mother handed each a bowl, and the children drank, the water running down their chins.

The birds were everywhere—flycatchers and jays and hummingbirds.

"What is the name of that bird?" she asked in Spanish, pointing to the brilliant red flycatcher.

"¡Mosquero!" shouted the boy.

"And the pretty blue one?" she said, pointing to the pinyon jay.

"¡Chara!" said the girl at once. *"¡Chara piñon!"*

Now all the birds began to circle them, singing to them happily and playing with their hair.

The mountains and the village faded and they were once more in the church. The mother looked down at the children in her arms. She rocked them gently, calling out their names. They did not answer her, nor did they move. The mother pulled them close to her. She leaned her head against the wall and looked up at the sky.

Against the sun, she saw the bird.

High above them, black as death, it circled. Never did its great wings move.

Suddenly its shadow passed across them all *"¡Halcón!"* the mother cried. *"Halcón satánico!"*

The devil's hawk had come.

ONE

"SEÑORES!...SEÑORAS!..." The leader of the mariachi band lifted his trumpet in the air. *"¡'La Cucaracha'!"*

The six men began to play. The crowd surrounding them applauded, while some children covered their ears. The leader turned and the band followed, marching down the center of the street, their huge sombreros bobbing as they went.

Jon Wilder watched them go. Then he, too, joined the others crowding the main street of Santa Rita. Forty miles south of Tucson and twenty-five from the Mexican border, the former mission settlement had become a favorite destination for the many who arrived in cars and tour buses, eager to explore the restored adobe buildings that contained the shops of local artisans and craftspeople.

Today the town was particularly popular. It was Saint Rita Day, named for its patron, Saint Rita of Cascia. According to the Catholic Church, the actual feast day of the saint was May 22. But on this afternoon in mid-June, no one seemed to care. Years ago, the town council had selected this date on which to hold one last spring festival before the oppressive heat of summer settled in. Although the temperature had risen above a hundred degrees several days that week, the tourists and day-trippers appeared unaffected as they ambled through the streets.

Jon Wilder was not a tourist. But like them he was dressed in casual light clothes. As he continued walking, he passed stalls advertising native crafts and streetside vendors selling tacos and fried bread. Everywhere there were elaborate displays of artificial flowers in a rainbow of bright colors—reds and purples, greens and blues. Peering into a courtyard, he saw a dozen children squealing at a blindfolded boy who was flailing at a large piñata hanging from the branches of a eucalyptus tree.

"Señor," a raspy voice called to him. *"Señor—por favor."*

Jon stopped. In an alleyway between two buildings a Mexican Indian woman sat on a metal lawn chair. Her age was impossible to guess. The eyes were rheumy, the whites a jaundiced yellow. What hair she had was white and pulled behind her in a braid. She had no teeth. In her lap she clutched what appeared to be the lower part of a large gourd that had been dried and hollowed out, so as to make a bowl. Inside it were several dozen dried and wrinkled chile pods.

"I tell your fortune, *sí?"* she said to Jon.

"No, gracias," Jon told her politely.

"Everyone must know their future, *señor,"* said the woman. "Only five dollars."

"Thank you. But I know mine. In the short term, anyway."

She gave a toothless smile. "Maybe there are some surprises for you still."

"All right." He handed her five dollars, which she tucked into the sleeve of her blouse.

She inclined her head and stared into the bowl, studying the chile pods, as a fortune-teller might read tea leaves. Then she raised the bowl and gave it a hard shake. She placed it on her lap again, murmured to herself, and gazed into it a second time.

"This I know," she said at last. "You have been visiting Arizona for some weeks. Tomorrow you are expecting to go back to your home in…" She paused. "Connect-tee-cut."

Jon was amused. "True. And does your bowl tell you why I've been in Arizona?"

"You have been studying the birds. And drawing them."

"True again," he said. But so far she hadn't demonstrated any real powers of clairvoyance. His visit to the area had been noted in several of the local newspapers, including his credentials as an ornithologist and well-known painter of birds. Photos of him had accompanied the articles. The woman probably recognized him as he passed her and decided he would be an easy mark.

"You've taken trips into the desert," she went on. "In search of birds."

"I have," he told her. "But you promised me you'd read my future."

"Yes," she said. She raised her head and studied

him in silence. Then she picked up the gourd, shook it, and set it on her lap. He saw her eyes grow small.

"Lo siento, Señor Wilder," she said. "I will not speak of what your future brings."

"Why not?"

"Some things are better not to know."

To his surprise, Jon felt a chill run through him. But he persisted. "What does the bowl tell you?"

Slowly her eyes rose to meet his. "You will die here among the birds. Now go," she told him. "Leave me."

"Ah, Jon! You're there!" he heard a man's voice call out.

Jon turned to see Emilio Flores coming toward him from across the street. Like Jon he was in his forties, a large bear of a man with luxuriant black eyebrows and a mustache that flowed downward at both ends, giving him the appearance of the revolutionary bandit Pancho Villa.

Stepping to the sidewalk, he gave Jon a broad smile. "I was afraid I'd lost you in the crowd."

Seeing the old woman, he nodded. *"Buenas tardes, señora."* He said something more to her in Spanish. She responded tersely, pulled the five-dollar bill from the sleeve of her blouse, and held it out.

She and Emilio continued their conversation. Throughout it, the woman shook her head.

Emilio glanced at Jon. "She wants you to take back the money you paid her."

Jon did so, and the two men began walking along the street.

"That was strange," Emilio said, after some moments. "Old Estella is something of a celebrity in Santa Rita. She's been telling fortunes since I was a small boy. Usually it's 'Give me five dollars, *por favor,* and I will promise you a long and happy life.' I've never seen her return money to anyone."

"Maybe it's because I'm not suppose to have a long and happy life," Jon said. "I'm supposed to die here among the birds."

Emilio shook his head, then chuckled. "Either she's gone loco or she needs more chile pods to shake. I've known you longer than she has, and *I* predict for you a long and happy life."

"I hope you're right."

The other stopped and took Jon's shoulders in his massive hands. "Tell me this. How many years have you and I been friends?"

"Twenty."

"Twenty. And every time you've come to Arizona, we have visited. You came to my wedding. You're godfather to our son. I think I know you well. Do you remember, the first time you came into my father's shop? Do you remember what you bought?"

"An onyx bird. A dove, I think."

"A white-winged dove," Emilio confirmed. "We talked about its habitat, its diet, and its call. The information fascinated you; you said later it was the beginning of your interest in the birds."

"It probably was."

"So since we have been friends for many years, I look ahead to many more. Forget Estella's gloomy prophecies. They're foolish. By tomorrow you'll be far away from here.''

Emilio gestured to the adobe building just ahead. The sign above the doors, in graceful scrollwork, said FLORES AND SON—IMPORTERS. People continued to pass in and out. "Excuse me if I speak briefly with my manager," he said. "On Santa Rita Day, the good saint blesses us with many sales." He held aside the door for two of woman with shopping bags, and went into the shop.

While Jon waited, he recalled the first meeting between them Emilio had spoken of. Emilio had been the "Son" of Flores and Son then. After his father's death, Emilio had managed it, building it into one of the most successful import-export businesses in that part of the state. Some had suggested that the name be changed. But Emilio maintained the hope that his own son, now ten, would eventually succeed him.

Emilio returned a short time later, chatting with an attractive Hispanic couple in their fifties. The man was tall and angular, with blacker hair than Jon had ever seen. The woman, too, was slim, her dark hair swept behind her in a bun, held by a turquoise and silver comb.

"Jon—I'd like you to meet Mr. and Mrs. Cardenal," Emilio said. "Nadia—Luis…this is Jon Wilder."

"The bird expert," Luis Cardenal said. "Then you're familiar with the Desert Museum west of Tucson. I find the aviary fascinating."

Jon nodded. "I make a point of visiting it every time I'm here."

The man turned his attention to Emilio. "We must be going. You'll inform me when you receive the Toltec figure."

"Certainly," Emilio assured him. "And I apologize for the delay. Customs officials are still holding it up on the Mexican side. As you know, the government is reluctant to part with archeological objects. But there's no question you're the rightful purchaser."

"There shouldn't be," Cardenal said crisply. "I paid the asking price and twice as much in bribes. Do what you can to expedite it."

"I will."

"Gracias." Cardenal took his wife's hand and the two of them continued down the street.

"Friends of yours?" Jon asked Emilio.

"Good customers, mostly," Emilio said as the couple disappeared among the crowd. "They moved here several years ago from Phoenix by way of Yuma. He's a bank executive in Tucson. His specialty is real estate. His wife is a cardiac surgeon."

He gave Jon a wry look. "Maybe the Toltec figure is for her."

"What do you mean?"

"The Toltecs were a tribe that came before the Aztecs. Like them, they often displayed images of human sacrifice in their art. Cardenal saw the figure at a shop in Ixtapalapa and asked me to acquire it for him as an importer. It's a reclining figure carved in stone and holding a receptacle. The receptacle was where the

Toltec priests placed the hearts of victims after they were killed.''

"Sounds like a charming piece to have around the house," Jon said.

Abruptly, from a nearby street, music could be heard; not the mariachi band, but a much larger group, enthusiastic if discordant, assaulting a John Philip Sousa march. Crowds that moments earlier had filled the street now hurried to the sidewalks.

"The parade's about to start," Emilio announced.

He and Jon stepped back against the building. Moments later, a Santa Cruz County sheriff's car, its roof lights flashing, came into view. It stopped, then began moving slowly along the street. Behind it came a marching band, its thirty or so members dressed in blue and yellow uniforms. On the side of the bass drum, in block letters, Jon saw the words SANTA RITA HIGH SCHOOL CABALLEROS. Behind the band, riding on a flatbed truck, were seven men whom Emilio identified as the mayor and town council. They were followed by a small fire truck from the Santa Rita Volunteer Fire Company. After them came groups of a half dozen or so people representing various local service organizations: the Chamber of Commerce, the Veterans of Foreign Wars, the Daughters of Geronimo, and Boy Scouts, Girl Scouts, Cub Scouts, and Brownies, all in their summer uniforms. Following them were decorated cars and pickup trucks promoting local businesses.

Finally, around the corner a vintage Ford Fairlane convertible appeared. The car was white with purple racing strips along the sides. Red, green, and white crepe paper streamers fluttered from the radio antenna. Perched on the top edge of the rear seat was a man in his mid-sixties who was decidedly Hispanic. He wore a flowered yellow shirt and dungarees, the knees of which had been worn through. In his right hand he waved an old straw hat with a frayed brim. His hair was long and dark and streaked with gray. But his most striking feature was his smile, dazzlingly white, which he lavished on the crowds.

"Who's that?" Jon asked. "He looks like an aging movie star."

"He's a star in his own right," Emilio told him. "That's Antonio Salera."

"The Salera who was the labor leader in the sixties?"

"The same. He's still a hero to a lot of migrant workers. Do you know his story?"

"He came here as an illegal," Jon said. "That much I remember."

"With no education and few skills. To get across the border, he hid inside the trunk of that car, dressed in the clothes he's wearing now. He puts them on for appearances like this. His audiences love it."

The convertible passed them and continued slowly down the street. Salera, waving the straw hat, turned and called out to a group of teenage girls, who shrieked in delight.

"He's still a charismatic figure," Jon said.

"And a potent force in Mexican American relations," Emilio added, "particularly when it comes to workers' rights. When Congress was debating the NAFTA treaty, he was called to Washington to testify. He lives near Tucson but spends a great deal of time raising money for AMIGOS.''

"What's AMIGOS?''

"An organization Salera founded several years ago. It stands for the Alliance for Mexican Immigrants Gaining Official Status. They assist Mexican aliens who've been living here illegally. AMIGOS helps them to get green cards and work papers. Some people think it's a front for the drug cartel. Either way Salera's still a controversial figure. To many he's a saint. Others would be just as glad if he were dead.''

As the parade ended, Emilio looked at his watch. "It's five o'clock. There's a call I must make. Why don't you wait in the sales room? Afterward, we can go together to the house. Maria is preparing a special dinner for your last night here.''

He opened a door and they entered the shop. Emilio headed toward his office at the rear. Jon remained in the large, central sales room and watched as shoppers came and went. On shelves and tables there were Mexican ceramics, weavings, crystal and jewelry in gold, silver, and copper, all of the fine quality that had earned Flores and Son its reputation. Behind the main room, near Emilio's office, Jon recalled there was a small section devoted to art and handicrafts that represented birds. Displayed were brightly painted roosters, parrots, and doves from Mexico in metal, clay, and papier-mâché as well as birds fashioned out of wood and stone. Jon made his way back to see if new items had been added.

He had begun examining the figure of an eagle carved from walnut when he heard Emilio speaking on the telephone. Although the office door was closed, the voice became angry, urgent. The man cursed in Spanish. The receiver was slammed down.

The office door swung open and Emilio appeared. His face was grim. Turning, he saw Jon. "What are you doing here?"

"I was looking at the birds." He paused. "Is something wrong?"

"No, no," Emilio insisted. "You took me by surprise." He waved. "Come. Follow me to the house," he said, and hurried toward the exit door.

TWO

DEEP SHADOWS clung to the walls of Mariposa Canyon when Jon awoke at dawn. He had packed his suitcases after returning from Emilio's home last night and could be on the road by seven, well before the heat became extreme.

He showered quickly, dried, and shaved. Studying the face reflected in the mirror, Jon realized he was far tanner now than when he'd first arrived. Two weeks in the Arizona sun had given him a bronzelike hue. There were the lines beside his mouth that told him he should smile more. Otherwise, he was reasonably pleased with what he saw; a tall man, with hazel eyes and thick, dark hair. His chin was sharp and cleft. Modesty aside, he thought he still looked younger than his years.

His demanding schedule of those two weeks could have tired him. But they had not. He had found each day had been demanding but invigorating. Spending time in the Sonoran desert always was. Years ago, before his wife had died, they'd come to Tucson and explored the mountains and the desert that surrounded it. To his surprise Jon found that in a climate many thought of as too harsh and arid, nature thrived.

Since then, he had returned many times, lecturing, conducting field trips, and, always, making notes and sketches of the birds he saw. Returning to Scarborough, Connecticut, where he maintained a large house on the shore, he would paint watercolor portraits of the birds using those sketches. Many of the paintings hung in galleries and in private collections. Others found their way into the pages of the nature guides that Jon created and that had earned him an enthusiastic audience.

He dressed and headed to the kitchen. As he waited for the coffee to brew, he picked up a stack of candid snapshots he had taken when he first arrived. One photo in particular showed Emilio the way Jon liked to think of him. It had been taken on a birding trip. In the photograph, Emilio and his wife, Maria, who was as petite as he was large, stood beneath a paloverde tree. Emilio was beaming at the camera, as if saying "Life is wonderful, enjoy it! *I* do!" Jon thought of how completely the man shared that love of life with everyone he knew.

It was not the man Jon saw last night. Throughout dinner, Emilio seemed anxious and distracted. Several times he had excused himself—to make a call, he said. In his absence, Maria had attempted to maintain a cheerful mood. But she, too, showed an undercurrent of concern. What they were concerned about was never said. But it hung over the evening like a shadow, darkening what should have been a festive visit.

As Jon was leaving, Maria offhandedly suggested he stop by in the morning for one last good-bye. Emilio had given her a sidelong glance but finally concurred. Jon had accepted. Now he wished he hadn't. For the first time in their friendship, he felt reluctant to see them until whatever was troubling them passed.

The kitchen clock showed 6:19 when Jon finished his breakfast. He carried the photographs into the living room and slipped them into an envelope, which he placed inside a suitcase. After returning to the kitchen with his suitcases, he poured himself a second mug of coffee. As he drank, he looked out through the sliding doors that opened on the patio. The house that he had rented from a local real estate agent had been ideal. High in the mountains above Santa Rita, it provided a stunning, panoramic view. Already the sun had touched the ridgeline of the mountains to the west. He slid apart the doors and stepped outside. Walking to the edge of the patio, he realized one thing he would miss most about the house was the view. A thousand feet below, the desert valley shimmered in an early morning glow. To the north, the lights of Tucson faded as the city waked. To the south, Nogales, Arizona, still slept on in a dusty haze, as did her similarly named sister-city of Nogales, Mexico.

Jon went back to the kitchen, picked up his suitcases, and carried them out to his car. He made a last trip to the house to make certain the doors and windows were secure. He left the house keys on the kitchen counter, as the rental lease instructed him.

Then he thought of Señor Liebre. He went to the refrigerator, found a few remaining lettuce leaves, and put them on a plate. He made a final visit to the patio.

As he did, a large jackrabbit hopped out from behind some shrubbery and stood staring at him with a look of hungry expectation. It had appeared the third day Jon was in the house, when Emilio was visiting. Emilio had named it Señor Liebre—*Liebre* was the Spanish word for hare. Since then it had come every day to eat whatever scraps of vegetables Jon left for it.

Jon set down the plate. "Good morning, Señor Liebre," he said.

The soft brown eyes of the rabbit blinked. Its ears twitched several times.

"I hate to tell you," Jon said, "but it's *adiós,* my friend. I'm leaving. Take care of yourself and watch out for coyotes."

Jon continued to his car. As he pulled out of the driveway, he saw the rabbit's nose was buried in the plate.

IN THE MORNING LIGHT, the community of Santa Rita seemed a ghost town after the color and excitement of the day before. Gone were the visitors and sightseers. The shops and businesses were shuttered, the streets silent and empty, the patios and cul de sacs deserted.

The Flores home was an attractive ranch house several miles east of the town. Like many of its neighbors, it was of adobe brick with a Spanish tile roof and ironwork designs on many of the windows, also in the Spanish style. Approaching it, Jon saw their car and the pickup truck Emilio used for his business parked in the carport. He was surprised to see Emilio beside the truck. The man looked as if he had had little sleep.

He was about to climb into the truck when Jon hailed him.

"I have to go. Excuse me," Emilio said at once.

Maria suddenly appeared on the walk leading from the house. "Emilio—let Jon go with you."

"No."

"What is it?" Jon looked first to Maria, then Emilio. "What's happened?"

"My sister, her family, and some others were expected yesterday from Mexico," Emilio said. "We think they were abandoned in the desert."

"Emilio is going to look for them," Maria put in.

"Let me go with you," Jon said.

"No," Emilio repeated firmly.

"I'll ride beside you in the truck," Jon persisted. "I can help look for them while you drive."

"Emilio—" Maria urged. "Take Jon with you."

Emilio regarded Jon in silence. Finally he nodded. "All right. Come."

THE PICKUP TRUCK drove west toward open desert. All the while, Emilio said nothing. Instead, he focused his attention on the narrow, twisting road. Jon asked no questions. But he was reasonably certain what had occurred.

They were nearing the small settlement of Esperanza when Emilio spoke. "My sister, Angélica, and her husband and their children were to be brought across the border yesterday. Also, a cousin and her son. Six in all."

"Were they entering illegally?" Jon asked him.

"Yes."

"Where?"

"I don't know. Somewhere west of Nogales, I think. The immigration people at the Nogales checkpoint have become very vigilant. So the smugglers cross in remote areas: the mountains or places in the desert where the terrain is difficult. They vary them to avoid the Border Patrol."

"Do the smugglers have a name?"

"They work in separate gangs, sometimes named for their leader. The smugglers themselves are called *coyotes,* like the mangy animals they are. They bring the people, usually in groups of six or eight, to pre-arranged locations on this side of the border. There they are met by others."

"Did you make the arrangements for them to be brought here?"

"Yes. A month ago, a man came into the shop," Emilio said. "He was Mexican. At first, I thought he was a customer. But when I asked if I could help him, he said it was he who could help me. He told me he knew I had someone I wished to bring into the United States. 'Unofficially,' as he put it. The truth is, I had been trying for a year to arrange visas for my sister and the others legally. They are my only family left. It was impossible."

"Was it red tape?"

"That, yes, and more. Three years ago, Angélica's husband was arrested by the Mexican police. The charge was assault. They said he beat a man. My brother-in-law told them the man who had accused him was a thief. He'd been discovered in their house. When he was confronted, the thief attacked my brother-in-law, who fought back and finally got the better of the man. The authorities were called. The thief, for his part, said he'd simply wandered into the wrong house by accident and been beaten without cause."

"And the police?"

"Publicly, they claimed they didn't know which story to believe. But they implied, not subtly, that money could tip the scales of justice either way. The thief bribed them handsomely; my brother-in-law wouldn't. So he was the one charged. The case never came to trial, but the record of his arrest made legal immigration very difficult. That was when I knew I had to use whatever means I could to get them out of Mexico."

"The man who visited you in your shop," Jon asked him. "What did he offer to do?"

"If I was interested and paid a certain fee, he said he would give me a number in Tucson to call. That person would arrange things. I paid and made the call that afternoon."

"You said it was yesterday they were to be smuggled in?"

"Before dawn, yes," Emilio confirmed. "Once here, *coyotes* on this side of the border were to take them to a house in Tucson. At five o'clock I was to call the number I'd been given and would be told where they could be picked up today."

"And when you called?"

"A recorded message said the number had been disconnected. I contacted the phone company. They checked their records and repeated that the number was no longer in service. That's when I knew something had gone very wrong. I called again several times last night when you were at the house. I kept hoping there was some mistake."

"So you decided to search for them this morning."

"I wanted to last night after you'd gone," Emilio said. "But in the desert with the darkness it would have been impossible."

"Where will you look now?"

"Several places. Each offers some protection from the sun. If they're out there I just pray they have found one of them." He returned his attention to the road.

Looking through the side window to his cab, Jon saw waves of heat were already rising from the desert floor. Midday temperatures the day before had been over 105 degrees. In the desert it could have been twenty degrees hotter. The same was expected for today.

Emilio began to slow the truck. Rounding a curve, Jon saw what appeared to be an old dirt road. Beyond it, rotten fence posts flanked the shoulders. Emilio brought the pickup to a halt. Nailed to a post was a rusted metal sign. The lettering on it was barely visible, but Jon could make out the words: DAVIS MINING COMPANY: H. AND S. DAVIS, OWNERS—TRESPASSERS KEEP OUT.

Emilio maneuvered the truck onto the dirt road. "One location the *coyotes* sometimes used was an old copper mine. It went out of business in the fifties, but there are still buildings.''

They jounced over the gullied road. Then in the distance, Jon saw the buildings Emilio had spoken of: three large structures of corrugated metal that could have served as offices and storage sheds. They might afford shelter. But as the sun beat down on them, temperatures inside would approach those of an oven.

Emilio swung the pickup truck around and stopped next to a building. ''I shouldn't be long. I don't see any signs of life.'' He climbed out and started toward it at a rapid pace.

Jon waited in the truck. Ten feet ahead, the land appeared to drop away to nothing. He left the cab and walked over to the edge. Gazing down, he saw the mine was vast and deep, with a narrow trail that spiraled to the bottom, as if a giant screw had been ground into the earth. A sense of vertigo began to seize him; he turned quickly and headed for the truck.

A moment later Emilio returned and climbed in beside him. ''I was wrong about no life in there,'' he said. ''It's full of rattlesnakes.''

He swung around the pickup truck again and they started back to the paved road. It led through desert scrub, studded with yucca, brittlebush and ocotillo, and a variety of cactus. Towering among them were the monarchs of the desert, the saguaro, some more than twenty feet in height.

Emilio reached under the seat and brought up a large Thermos. He offered it to Jon. ''It's water. Care for some?''

"No, thanks."

"You'll change your mind. A person needs six quarts a day to function in the summer. Two gallons, if you're out of doors. The Spanish missionaries called this part of the desert *las arenas del fuego,* the sands of fire."

Emilio drank deeply, replaced the lid, and put the Thermos on the seat between them.

Driving south, the sun now beat directly at the windshield with such intensity even the sunglasses Jon was wearing seemed inadequate.

"Maybe I'll have some water, after all," he said.

Emilio handed him the Thermos, at the same time giving him an I-told-you glance. Jon took several swallows, feeling the cool liquid trickle down his throat. At that moment, something caught his eyes.

He shaded them with a hand and leaned forward for a better view. He lost the object briefly in the sun, then saw it reappear.

"What are you looking at?" Emilio asked, curious.

"A bird. At least, I think it is," Jon told him. "Very large and dark. It's soaring on the thermals."

Emilio frowned. "A turkey vulture. Even in the desert, scavengers like them always find a meal. It's probably feeding on the carcass of an animal."

"Is there anything in that direction?"

"No. That way is barren desert. Nothing's there. Well, almost nothing. There's the remains of an old church."

"A church?"

"A mission," Emilio said. "It was built soon after Father Kino and the Spanish missionaries came."

"I thought most of the old mission churches in the area had been restored."

"Not that one. It was cursed."

Jon looked at him. "What do you mean, cursed?"

"When the Jesuits built the missions, many young priests were assigned to them. Unfortunately, the *padre* who'd been sent to that one lost his mind. Maybe it was loneliness or homesickness or more heat than he could bear. He started celebrating black masses in the devil's name. One of his 'sacraments' was to violate young girls on the altar during services, as worshippers looked on in shock. Soon the friendly Indians who'd been converted to Christianity conspired with the settlers. They killed the priest, then sacked the church and burned it to the ground."

"Was it ever used as a dropping off place for illegals?"

"Never. Even the smugglers don't want anything to do with it."

Jon saw the bird again. It was a turkey vulture, certainly. A thousand feet above, it circled effortlessly, almost lazily, on long, extended wings. Now and then, it would drop suddenly and disappear from sight, then rise again.

Emilio was now watching it, as well. The same thought seemed to be forming in his mind as it had in Jon's.

"Maybe we should have a look anyway," Emilio said.

He let the pickup truck glide off the road, onto the hard, uneven shoulder and, finally, onto a trail not much wider than the truck itself. They climbed a rise. Once over it, the terrain became extremely rough. They descended to a low, flat desert basin dominated by saguaros, climbed another rise, and stopped. A hundred yards ahead there were the ruins of the church. Facing them, they saw what once had been a wall. In the center was an opening.

Emilio drove slowly to the wall and stopped the pickup truck again. Both men climbed out.

Emilio moved toward the opening. Jon followed a short distance behind. On the lintel stone above the opening, Jon saw a Latin cross. Stepping through the opening, Emilio stood for a few moments, looking at the sky.

Then he took another step and turned.

An anguished cry exploded from his chest. He fell, collapsing to his knees, his hands clutching his face.

Jon rushed to him—and saw now what Emilio had seen.

A young woman in a white dress lay with her back against the wall. A look of terror filled her eyes. At her side, held tightly in her arm, was a small boy. Cradled in her other arm, there was a girl.

All were dead.

THREE

THE ROOF LIGHTS of the vehicles pulsed, urgent and incongruous, against the pale blue-white of the sky.

Jon watched as the ambulance carrying the bodies of Emilio's sister and her children drove away, escorted by a county sheriff's car. Two other sheriff's department cars remained parked at oblique angles near the wall of the mission, as officers examined the area for evidence. Around the area, yellow police tape swayed languidly in the hot, morning breeze.

A short distance away, a young Hispanic man in a green Border Patrol uniform was kneeling in the rear of Emilio's pickup truck, as if he, too, were searching for evidence.

Emilio sat with his head bowed in the front seat of a Ford Expedition, white with blue trim, the words "U.S. Border Patrol" visible along the side. Beside him was an older man, also dressed in a Border Patrol uniform. His arm was around Emilio's shoulder and he was talking quietly, as if providing comfort and support.

At last, the officer stepped out of the Expedition and walked toward Jon. The man was short and muscular, with close-cropped sandy hair. Aviator-style sunglasses covered his eyes. As he reached Jon, he offered out his hand.

"Mr. Wilder?" the man said. "Agent Stuart Van Dine, United States Border Patrol, Tucson sector."

The two shook hands.

"First, I can't tell you how sorry I am," Van Dine began. "This sort of thing is never easy, but it's worse when there are kids. How old were the boy and girl?"

"Six and eight, I think."

Van Dine shook his head and spat into the sand, then pointed to the pickup truck where the other agent had begun taking photographs. "That's Agent Martinez," he indicated. "I know he spoke with Mr. Flores, but I'd like to ask you a few questions also."

"Of course."

"You don't look like you're from this area. Just visiting?"

"Just visiting," Jon said. "I'd planned to leave today."

"Going where?"

"To Phoenix, first. Then north to Sedona and maybe the Grand Canyon. My home is in Connecticut."

"You've been in Arizona on vacation?"

"Not really. I study birds and paint them."

"Was it you who contacted the authorities?"

"Yes. Mr. Flores was too upset. After I got him back to the truck, I used my cell phone to call."

"Who discovered the bodies by the wall?"

"He found them first. I'm told it was originally a group of six. There was a man, the woman's husband,

plus another woman and her son but they don't seem
to be here."

"We know," the agent said. "A Border Patrol air-
craft spotted the bodies of the man and the boy east
of here. They'd probably gone in search of help, or
maybe water, when their luck ran out."

"And the other woman?" Jon asked.

"The sheriff's people found her near a highway.
Naked. The heat must have given her hallucinations.
Apparently, she ripped off pieces of her clothing as
she went. Her body was faceup in a ditch."

Disgust was etched on Van Dine's face. "It would
have been kinder if the smugglers had shot them when
they had the chance. Instead, they left them here to
die like this. In the summer, the desert can get as hot
as a hundred forty degrees. I grew up in Minnesota
freezing my ass off most of the winter. Days like this
I wish I was back."

"Who do you think did this?" Jon asked him.

"We have four gangs operating in our sector who
regularly smuggle aliens. For three of them it's strictly
business. Cash and carry. Pay 'em cash, they carry
aliens across the border with no questions asked. The
fourth group is a bunch of vicious sons of bitches. It's
my guess they're the ones responsible for this."

He thrust out a hand to Jon again. "Anyway, thanks
for your time, Mr. Wilder."

"Before you go," Jon said, "may I ask you a few
questions, also?"

Van Dine looked puzzled. "About what?"

Jon gestured toward the Hispanic agent. He was still

examining the pickup truck. "Mr. Flores told me that when Agent Martinez first questioned him, he treated Mr. Flores as if he were implicated in the crime."

"If he did that, I apologize," Van Dine allowed. "Martinez is Mexican, and I'm not crazy about Mexicans in general. But the bureau has a quota, so we took him on as a trainee. Also, he's not the fastest bullet in the chamber, if you know what I mean. I'll speak to him."

Van Dine paused. "On the other hand, your friend, Mr. Flores, paid money to criminals to smuggle his sister and the others into the United States. If the INS decided to play hardball, they could prosecute. He's still a suspect, whether that makes him uncomfortable or not. Maybe something in the deal went awry between him and the smugglers. Maybe Mr. Flores threatened to tip off the authorities. Who knows?"

"None of those things happened," Jon said. "I'm quite sure."

Van Dine shrugged. He looked unconvinced.

"I have another question," Jon went on. "When will the bodies be released?"

"Tomorrow, or the day after," Van Dine said. "They'll be taken to the morgue in Tucson. Why do you ask?"

"This will be a tough time for the Flores family. I've been thinking of staying awhile longer and being whatever help to them I can."

"I thought you were leaving today."

"I may change my mind."

Van Dine inclined his head, obviously studying Jon

through his dark glasses. They were interrupted by the arrival of Martinez. He was carrying a cell phone in his hand.

"Sir—a call," the agent told Van Dine.

"Who is it?"

"Your deputy."

"Montoya?"

"Yes, sir."

"Excuse me," Van Dine said to Jon. He took the phone. "Yes, Max…I'm leaving now… No. Wait for me at headquarters. I'll be there in an hour. We'll talk then."

He handed the phone back to Martinez. Then he turned to Jon again. "It's up to you whether you stay or not. But if you do stay, don't get mixed up in this case. As I said, Flores could be implicated in the smuggling. And you don't want to be considered an accessory."

He and Martinez started back in the direction of their vehicle. Seeing them, Emilio stepped out. Van Dine passed him without acknowledgment. The two agents climbed into the vehicle and drove away. Emilio and Jon watched them depart.

Jon came to him. "I guess we're free to go. Would you like me to drive?" he asked, noticing the keys Emilio was holding in his hand.

The other shook his head. "No. I'm all right."

He looked at Jon. Grief filled his eyes. "Angélica was wearing a white dress. My sister was."

"I know."

"I gave that dress to her. Last week when we spoke,

she told she would be wearing it the next time we met." Emilio began to sob.

Jon took the keys, put an arm around the shoulder of his friend, and led him to the truck.

THE BELLS OF St. Anne's Church sounded two o'clock as Jon parked his car along the street. On their return to Santa Rita, Emilio said he hoped to see the priest that afternoon and make arrangements for the funeral. Other than that, the man was mostly lost in his own thoughts. The few times he spoke it was to recall memories of Angélica and their early years in Mexico. Twice Jon offered to help in any way he could. Emilio had thanked him and said nothing more.

Jon climbed the stone steps of the church and pushed aside the wooden doors. The vestibule was cool and dimly lit, as was the nave beyond. There were no windows along either side. Still, the white stucco walls glowed with a soft luminescence that was welcoming and warm. In the transept to the left novena candles burned beneath a statue of the Virgin Mary. High up on the columns at each side of the altar, winged angels in brightly colored tunics gazed down with placid eyes.

Looking in the direction of the altar, Jon saw Emilio and a second figure he assumed to be the priest talking quietly in a front pew. As Jon started toward them, Emilio turned his head and rose.

"Oh, Jon, I'm glad you're here." He gestured to the priest. "Father Francisco—this is Jon Wilder. The father and I were discussing details of the funeral."

The priest stood, facing Jon. He was somewhat younger than Jon, with a round face and curly reddish hair. In spite the Spanish name Emilio had given him, Father Francisco was unquestionably Irish. What Jon also realized from the dark glasses the priest wore and the white cane lying on the pew was that the man was blind.

The priest offered his hand. "I'm delighted to meet you, Mr. Wilder. By the way, most of the Hispanic members of my congregation call me Father Francisco. But officially, I'm Father Francis Matthew Flannery, S.J."

The two shook hands.

"Is there any more that I can tell you, Father?" Emilio inquired of the priest.

"Possibly one thing. If you provide me with the names of the lullabies, the *canciónes de cuna,* your sister sang to her children, I may be able to include them in the service."

"Yes, thank you. I will." Emilio held up a small leather-covered missal. "And thank you for providing this. I'm sure the service will be what my sister would have wished."

He glanced at Jon. "You're welcome to come back to the shop with me. But I still have calls to make."

"If Mr. Wilder has the time, I'd be pleased if I could have a word with him myself," the priest said. He turned to Jon. "I'm a birder, also, and a great admirer of your books. I was regretting that I missed your visit here. I only returned last night from a trip. Do you have a few minutes?"

"Certainly," Jon said.

"Come to the shop when you're done," Emilio told Jon. "I'll be there." He thanked the priest again and left the church.

Father Flannery touched the face of his wristwatch, feeling the raised numerals. "It's almost two-fifteen. Would you care for some iced tea?"

"That sounds fine."

"Good. We'll have it in the courtyard. It's shaded, and for some reason beyond human understanding, God blesses it with a delightful breeze even on the hottest days. Please follow me."

The priest led them through a door at the far end of the transept, holding his cane but without touching the tip to the floor. Even with his blindness, Jon decided, Father Flannery knew every square foot of the church and probably the surrounding grounds, as well.

They emerged into a lovely courtyard, mostly covered by a ramada of roughhewn wood, interlaced with bougainvillea. Lemon and fig trees separated the courtyard from a small flower garden beyond. In the center of the courtyard, a fountain ringed with Spanish tiles splashed. Small birds flitted to the edge of it, drank quickly, and flew off.

Father Flannery waved to a pair of heavy wooden armchairs. A low wooden table faced them. "Sit, please," he said. "And may I call you Jon?"

"I hope you will."

They sat. The priest picked up a small bell from the table and rang it. Moments later, a pretty, dark-haired girl in her early twenties appeared from an adjacent building.

"*¿Padre…?*" the girl asked.

"Gloria—*Éste es Señor Wilder*. Jon this is Gloria," he said. *"Té con hielo,"* he went on in perfect Spanish. He held up two fingers. *"Dos. Por favor."*

The girl nodded and returned quickly to the building.

"As I told you," Father Flannery continued, "I enjoy your books very much. Gloria reads them to me in the evening. She also describes the paintings of the birds. For instance, your use of color in the picture of the western meadowlark. The vivid yellow on the throat and breast is wonderful."

"Thank you," Jon said. "You also mentioned you were a birder."

The priest smiled. "Bird *listener* would be more accurate. Sometimes I record them. I have equipment in my study that lets me listen to the sounds they make. Over the years, I think I've developed an ability to identify birds by their calls. I'll demonstrate right now."

He pointed to the fig tree. "Sitting on the upper branches of the fig tree is a curved-bill thrasher. You can hear the *whit-wheet* sound it's making. Am I right?"

Acknowledging the introduction, the bird looked down and squawked its presence like a loud and pushy guest.

Jon smiled at his host. "It wouldn't surprise me if your congregation called you St. Francis."

"The children have another name for me. In my priest's outfit, I am *el mirlo*—the blackbird. Sometimes *el mirlo ciego*—the blackbird who is blind."

"Did you grow up in Arizona?"

"South Boston," the priest answered. "After I was ordained, I was assigned a small parish in the Midwest. But soon—how shall I put it?—I found myself in disagreement with the hierarchy of my diocese. I was considered much too liberal, particularly where the rights of women were concerned. Had it been fifteenth-century Spain, I'm sure the Grand Inquisitor would have personally burned me at the stake. Even so, the bishop gave me a choice: publicly repudiate the things I'd said or accept a parish that was so distant and so tiny that my heresy would not be heard."

"Was that how you came to Santa Rita?"

"Yes. And my blindness notwithstanding, these have been the happiest years of my life."

He inclined his head and listened. "Ah—I think I hear our iced tea on its way."

A moment later, Gloria reappeared bearing a tray with two tall glasses of iced tea. In the fleeting glance she gave the priest, Jon thought he knew another reason for the man's happiness. Jon took a glass as the tray was put before him; Father Flannery, the other.

"*Gracias,*" the priest said to her.

"*De nada, Padre.*" She gave him a demure nod and left the courtyard with the tray.

Father Flannery now raised his glass in a salute. "In addition to my admiration for you as an artist, I also wanted to say thanks."

"For what?"

"For being such a good friend to Emilio. He said that after finding the bodies of his sister and her children, you offered to help him any way you could."

"That's right."

"He also said you'd originally planned to leave today."

"I had. My idea was to travel for a few weeks in northern Arizona," Jon said. "But I'm not on any schedule. I can just as well spend the time here."

"Spend it how?" Father Flannery asked. "Digging into who's responsible for leading Emilio's sister and the others to their deaths? Emilio told me you were successful solving several other crimes when the police could not."

"Maybe. But I don't pretend I'm a detective. My way of gaining information is more patient and more subtle than theirs. Often the police are under pressure to solve crimes and make arrests as quickly as they can. I'm not. I look for answers the same way a birder looks for birds that hide in undergrowth. I watch for small details others might ignore. If I can do something to discover who's behind the deaths of those six people, then I will."

Father Flannery was silent. Instead, he turned his face in the direction of the mountains, as if lost in thought. "There was a young man years ago who felt the same as you," he said at last. "He was outraged at the vicious treatment of the aliens by smugglers. The robbery. The rapes of women. Leaving them to die excruciating deaths. Like you, he was an idealist.

He wanted to see justice done. He began asking questions, seeking the identities of those responsible.''

"Did he succeed?''

"Indeed he did. Because of him, one of the most notorious smugglers in this part of the country was identified, along with several in his gang. With testimony the young man provided, they were convicted and sentenced to life terms. Justice had been served. Case closed. But not entirely. The day after the trial ended, two members of the gang who'd managed to elude police kidnapped the young man and shot him in the head.''

He paused. "The bullet didn't kill him, though,'' the priest told Jon. "It left him blind.''

FOUR

HAVE YOU CAUGHT THE COTTONWOOD SPRINGS SPIRIT?

THE WORDS SANG ACROSS the billboard in bold letters. Below them was the picture of a gray-haired man and woman grinning at the driver as he passed. They were lounging on a patio, drinks in one hand, golf clubs in the other. Both were deeply tanned and in spite of their gray hair seemed so vigorous and youthful, they could have been the AARP poster couple of the year.

A mile past the billboard, Jon swung off the interstate and turned onto Fountain of Youth Boulevard, which, he discovered, was the main thoroughfare of the retirement community itself.

After leaving the church and stopping briefly at the shop to see Emilio, it had occurred to Jon that he no longer had a place to live. His rental on the house in Mariposa Canyon had expired; he had locked the doors with the keys sitting on the kitchen countertop.

Jon continued along Fountain of Youth Boulevard, until he saw a set of arrows indicating Desert Vistas Mall. He turned in, avoiding a clutch of senior citizens in golf carts filled with grocery bags, and maneuvered through the parking lot until he found a space. Directly opposite, he saw the sign for Cottonwood Springs Realty. He left his car and walked to it.

The broker's office, as he entered, appeared typical. Photographs of houses lined the walls, along with certificates of merit from one organization or another and a board where current listings had been posted.

What was not typical was the figure sprawled behind the desk. The man wore an avocado-colored leisure suit. He lay back in his chair; his snakeskin boots were crossed and resting on the desk. His face was hidden behind a copy of *Guns and Ammo* magazine.

When the man lowered the magazine and turned, Jon saw the rest of him. He was vast, his face and hands the shade and texture of rawhide long exposed to desert sun. A bolo tie with a large turquoise set in silver hung around the neck.

"Howdy," the man said. "Billy Ketchum at your service." He stood up and beamed. "And you are?"

"Jon Wilder."

The name appeared to have no meaning. "Well, if you're figuring to locate in Cottonwood Springs, I'll have to tell you 'sorry.' This is a retirement community. Over fifties only. You look too young to make the cut."

"I rented a house from you in Mariposa Canyon," Jon reminded him. "The lease was up today. But if you don't have another renter coming in, I'd like to stay awhile longer."

"Wilder—Jon Wilder," The name was jogging Ketchum's memory. "Oh, yeah, you called me from back east a couple months ago. You draw or something, don't you?''

"Yes.''

"I'll get the file.''

The man walked to a set of cabinets against the wall and found the drawer that he was looking for. He pulled it out, riffled among folders, and selected one.

"Wilder, Jonathan M.,'' he said to himself, flipping pages.

He returned to the desk, sat, and began looking through the contents, when the telephone rang. "Hold on,'' he told Jon, and grabbed up the receiver. "Cottonwood Springs Realty, Billy Ketchum at your—'' The face clouded. "When?…How many?…Where?…Damn! God*damn!*…call me tonight. After eight…. *Sí. Sí.*'' The phone slammed down.

Billy Ketchum took a breath. "Sorry about that little bit of business there,'' he offered. "So, where were we? Yeah, the house in Mariposa Canyon.''

He went back to the folder briefly. Looking up at Jon again, the hail-fellow attitude returned.

"Shouldn't be a problem with you staying on,'' he said. "The owner lives in Michigan and only comes a couple months a year, January to May, generally. Snowbirds almost never stay beyond that. Hell, nobody wants to visit us in summer, and a lot who live here wish they had a chance to leave. Hot days like these, you need oven mitts to drive your car.''

Ketchum closed the folder. "Anyhow, the house is yours. Stop by again when you decide to leave.''

"My problem is I locked the house before I left. I left the keys inside."

"Don't worry. There's another set right here." Ketchum ripped away a small plastic bag stapled to the folder, opened it, took out some keys and tossed them on the desk.

"Otherwise, you know the terms," the agent went on. "No children and no pets."

"The only pet, if you can call him that, is a jackrabbit that visits me everyday for food."

Ketchum chuckled. "As long as he's not livin' in the house and droppin' all his rabbit do-do, it's allowed."

"Would you like a check now for the extra week?"

"I still have your security deposit," Ketchum said. "When you know how much more time you're gonna spend, we'll settle up."

He paused. "And one more thing. I better mention it. The owner's got this dislike about Mexicans; he doesn't even like 'em visiting the house. He wanted me to put in the lease I wouldn't rent to 'em. I said I couldn't do that; it's against the law. Still, I understand his feelings."

"What do you mean?"

"The border is a sieve. The Mexies keep on streaming through, and no one's gonna stop 'em, least of all those Keystone Cops in their green uniforms. They even got this thing called Operation Sandstorm. It's supposed to slow 'em down. It hasn't yet. Everyday you hear about illegals diggin' tunnels, cuttin' fences, hidin' in the trunks of cars. One guy even had his brothers shoot him over in some sort of giant sling-shot. It was good news, bad news. The slingshot worked, he flew over the border sure enough, but landed headfirst in a cactus. It was not a pretty sight.

"But don't misunderstand," Ketchum added. "I like Mexicans myself." He spread his hands to show his magnanimity. "Fact is, I got a Mexican girl who does housework for me twice a week. Her name's Chiquita—Chiquita Banana I call her. She has a husband and some kids in Veracruz; she's saving every cent she earns to bring 'em into the United States." He let out another laugh. "I help her, too. I give her extra money for what I call 'extra services.'"

Jon rose. "Excuse me, but if we're done, I'd like to get back to the house."

"Sure, sure, go ahead." Ketchum stood, as well. "If there's something I forgot, I'll call."

"Please do." Jon started for the door, then paused. On the wall was an object that he hadn't noticed earlier. It was a massive bullwhip. Black and coiled, it had plaited lashes at the tip splayed out, so as to suggest the pain they could inflict.

Ketchum saw it had caught Jon's attention. "That's one fine piece of leatherwork, now don't you think?" He gazed at it with admiration. "Truth be told, I used to be called Bullwhip Billy Ketchum. I was the youngest bullwhip champion in Loving County, Texas. Won all kinds of prizes as a boy. That whip I bought me when I moved to Arizona twenty years ago. I can still hit a bird in flight from twenty feet away." He laughed. "You oughta see the feathers fly." He turned to Jon again for his response.

But Jon was gone.

THE COFFINS, two of them small and white, were lowered slowly into the sandy earth. When they were covered over and the ground made smooth and flat again, flowers were placed next to the white wooden crosses marking them. The priest said the prayers of interment in both Spanish and English, and commended the souls of the four to everlasting life.

Standing at a distance from the graves, Jon studied the family as they mourned—Emilio, his face frozen in grief; Maria, weeping softly; their children, Nydia and Alejandro, both expressionless, uncomprehending of the depth of loss their parents shared.

There were about twenty other friends and neighbors of the Floreses gathered in the cemetery. There had been many more at the funeral, crowding the small church. When the service ended they had moved into the center aisle, filing slowly toward the front doors, where Emilio and his wife and the priest stood. Murmuring condolences, some lingered to express quiet words of comfort; others had shaken Emilio's hand or kissed Maria on the cheek.

The graveside service ended with a prayer from Father Flannery. Again, those who were there shook Emilio's hand and kissed Maria's cheek. Walking from the cemetery, some glanced briefly at the graves. The rest walked briskly toward the street, relieved the sad event was done.

When the last of them had left, Emilio came to Jon. "You'll be at the house, as well, I hope."

"Yes. Certainly."

"One thing, if I may ask," Emilio said. "The young woman who looks after the rectory, Gloria, she drives the father's car when he's in need of traveling. Regrettably, a family illness called her away today. Perhaps, if you don't mind—"

"I'd be delighted to bring Father Flannery in my car," Jon assured him.

"Thank you."

Father Flannery now joined them. "And thank you from me, too."

"You and Maria and the children go," Jon told Emilio. "We'll be there soon."

Emilio nodded, returned to where his wife and children waited, and the four walked slowly from the cemetery.

"I do appreciate it, Jon," the priest repeated. "Not only is Gloria my eyes, she's my wheels. Last night, an aunt who lives in Gila Bend was taken to the hospital. I urged Gloria to use the car." He motioned with his cane in the direction of the rectory. "Let me change out of these vestments. I'll meet you by the side entrance of the church."

"That's fine."

Father Flannery tilted his head back, as if studying the sky. "I'll bring an umbrella, also. I suspect we'll have rain soon."

Jon looked up also. Thunderheads were building in the west. "You may be right. How did you know?"

The priest smiled. "I could tell you it was divine inspiration, but I had a different sign. During the graveside service, I could hear the birds flying low to the ground, suggesting rain. Some think it's an old wives' tale, but I've found it to be true. I'll be with you shortly."

LOW-FLYING BIRDS or not, Father Flannery had been correct. As Jon waited for him near the church, billowing white clouds filled the sky, obscuring the sun. By the time the priest rejoined him, large, languid drops of rain were splattering the windshield of Jon's car.

"The monsoon season is beginning," Father Flannery said. "This part of Arizona gets eleven inches of rain a year. And most of it comes in late June and July, sometimes at the rate of three inches an hour. Last year one of my parishioners was driving home when his car stalled at a low place in the road and a flash flood swept them away. He was found in an arroyo two days later, still in the car, drowned."

"At least it held off until the service ended."

The priest nodded. "It was sad enough without the rain."

"About the funeral," Jon said. "There was a man most of the congregation seemed to know. I mean, his presence didn't go unnoticed."

"Oh? Describe him."

"Late fifties. Very tall and blond."

"That was Eric Voss," the priest informed him. "He made his money in the oil exploration business, mostly overseas. When his fortune was assured, he devoted himself entirely to environmental causes. I'm sure you've heard of Terravita."

"Certainly. What did the newspapers call it?—'A World Under Glass.'"

"A description that hardly does it justice," the priest said. "It's Voss's pleasure dome. Few outsiders are invited to visit, but I was there once on pastoral matters. A worker became gravely ill and insisted I be called to perform last rites."

"From the pictures of it, it looks vast."

"It is. Inside all that glass and steel are examples of most of the planet's ecosystems, each naturally re-created and maintained."

"When it was built, didn't people accuse Voss of being crazy?"

The priest laughed. "When you're as rich as Voss you're considered an eccentric visionary, not a loon. But his life has been, shall we say, unique. He's been married and divorced five times. When he became the white knight of the environmental movement, he led a seagoing armada that escorted the gray whales down the California coast."

"Greenpeace did the same," Jon said.

"Except Voss has a lot more green that Greenpeace does. And his boats were armed with surface-to-surface missiles to discourage whalers. It earned Voss a lot of 'Save the Whale' bumper stickers, I can tell you that."

"How is it he knows Emilio?" Jon asked.

"He's the largest contributor to the Santa Rita Audubon chapter. They met when Emilio was its president.''

They turned onto the road that led to the Flores home. Ahead, lines of cars were parked along both sides. Jon pulled over and switched off the wipers and the engine. The rain was now torrential, and small pellets of hail beat a noisy tattoo against the car.

''Let's wait a minute and hope that it lets up,'' Father Flannery suggested. He reached down for his umbrella on the floor.

''There was another person I noticed at the funeral,'' Jon said after a moment. ''A woman.''

The priest turned his head. ''Oh? Describe her.''

''She was young. Hispanic, also, and quite pretty.''

''There are a number of young women in Santa Rita who fit that description,'' Father Flannery said. ''Maybe she was a friend of the Floreses.''

''That's what I thought at first. She came in after the service began and stood in the rear of the church the entire time. The church was crowded, but I was in the last row and there were seats available. Also, the minute it was over, she left by a side door.''

''She could have been a tourist who happened to wander in and didn't want to look conspicuous.''

''Possibly,'' Jon said. ''But there was something else that puzzled me. During the service, she seemed less interested in what was going on than on certain people who were there.''

Jon added, ''I was one of them.''

ENTERING THE Flores home, Jon saw the living room was filled with people, many of whom had been in the church. Emilio suddenly appeared and took Father Flannery's umbrella. "Good. I'm glad both of you are here. Some wine? Maria also made some punch."

Jon chose a tonic; Father Flannery did the same. Emilio placed the umbrella with others in a stand in the foyer and disappeared among the guests.

As Jon and the priest stepped into the room, large hands clasped down on the priest's shoulders. The voice that spoke was distinctly Scandinavian. "Ah, Father Flannery—is it true the Pope made you Archbishop of Santa Rita?"

"That's right, Eric," Father Flannery said, turning. "Would you like to kiss my ring?"

The man laughed heartily, then stepped in front of them and seized Jon's hand. "I'm Eric Voss," he said. "And you're Jon Wilder, of course."

"Of course," Jon said.

"I'm a great admirer of yours," continued Voss. "I own a number of your watercolor portraits of desert birds. How long will you be in Arizona?"

"I'm not certain."

"Well, before you leave, you must visit Terravita. You know of it, I'm sure."

"I do."

"Visitors are not permitted," Voss said. "But I make exceptions for certain people whose credentials I approve. And I approve of yours. You'll be particularly interested in some of the rare bird species I've acquired."

"Thank you. I'd like to, if I have the time."

"Make time," Voss said. "My assistant, Miss Chimayo, will call you to specify a day and hour. Good day, gentlemen." He turned and walked away.

"You've just been given an offer you can't refuse," Father Flannery said wryly.

"It sounded more like an order," Jon said. "But I've wanted to see Terravita for a long time."

Emilio returned with glasses of tonic for the two and they continued into the room. For a half hour they mingled and chatted with other guests. Then, once more, Emilio came toward them. He told Father Flannery that Gloria had called and wished to speak with him. The priest excused himself and left the room. He returned soon after.

"Gloria was able to get back sooner than she thought," he said. "She offered to pick me up and drive me to the rectory. She's on her way. Do you mind if I go with her?"

"Not at all," Jon told him.

"We'll talk again, I hope. Thank you for the ride." The two shook hands and Father Flannery joined a couple who were headed toward the door. Others in the crowd began to follow. As people departed, Jon could see through the open door that rain was still deluging the walkway and the road. At the far side of the room, Maria was gathering up empty plates and glasses. Emilio was nowhere to be seen.

Jon approached her. "May I give you a hand?" he asked.

"Thank you, but no." She gave him a sad smile.

"Where's Emilio?"

"In the bedroom."

"Is he all right?"

She nodded and went on stacking plates.

"Would he mind if I spoke with him?"

"I'm sure not. You're a friend," Maria said.

Jon left the living room and walked down a hallway to the Floreses' bedroom. The door was closed. He knocked on it.

"Emilio—it's Jon. May I came in?"

There was silence, then a dull "yes."

Jon opened the bedroom door. Emilio sat on the side of the bed; his head was lowered and his hands were on his knees. "I'm sorry," he began. "It's just—all that's happened. And the weight of it…" He let his voice trail off.

Jon sat down on the bed. "Is there something I can do?"

"Others have asked me the same question. Some of our friends have offered to post a reward for finding the killers. They also said—and I agree with them— that the police may, or say they've tried, but no one will be caught."

"You're sure of that?"

"In Mexico, we grew up with distrust of the *judiciales,* the federal police. We feared them, in fact. Many were corrupt. Their pay is poor, so they depend on bribes. Here, most police are honest, conscientious. But when it comes to stopping those who smuggle aliens, they're overwhelmed. Streams of illegals cross the border into this country, day and night. The border between Mexico and the U.S. is very long. Last year, more than a hundred died of heat exposure in the desert, some locked in railcars, others left abandoned like my sister. Of the smugglers who guided them, few were ever caught. Even when they do catch someone, they're the small fry. The big fish always get away."

"You said you spoke to a man in Tucson who said he would arrange to bring the six people into the United States. Does this man have a name?"

"Victor."

"No last name?" Jon asked him.

"He didn't given one," Emilio said. "And I'm sure the Victor was an alias."

"What did he tell you it would cost?"

"Twelve hundred dollars a head; that was the phrase he used. This Victor even made a joke of it. He said for that price he would deliver not only the heads, but the rest of the bodies, too."

"How was the money to be paid?"

"About five miles north of here," Emilio said, "there was a community called Wyatt's Spur. It no longer exists, but the exit off the interstate is still marked with that name. Close to the exit is a restaurant called the King Toro Steakhouse."

"I know it," Jon said. "You can see it from the interstate. The place with the giant cattle horns and crown."

"Yes. Set around the parking lot in front are trash barrels made from oil drums. Victor instructed me to arrive there before six a.m. and go to the barrel at the south end of the lot. If I tipped the barrel, I would see a small depression in the earth. I was to place the money in the hole and put the drum over it again, so it could not be seen."

"The money was in cash?"

Emilio nodded. "Hundred-dollar bills, inside dark plastic covering and wrapped with tape."

"Do you know who retrieved the money after you'd hidden it?"

"No. I was told to leave the parking lot at once. But I know it got into Victor's hands. He confirmed it when I talked to him that afternoon. He thanked me and said he would make arrangements for transporting my sister and the others."

"And he was to call you again when they were safely in the United States."

"Yes," Emilio said. "You know the rest."

"Did you report all this to the police after the bodies were found?"

"Yes. And to the Border Patrol." Emilio's eyes took on a look of hopelessness. "I can do nothing more."

Jon was silent. But an idea was forming in his mind.

FIVE

THE HORNS, thirty feet across from tip to tip and surmounted with a gilded crown, gleamed in the early morning light. They were becoming a familiar landmark. Twice before Jon had made the trip just before dawn without success. As he approached along the highway access road, he saw the restaurant. It was a long, single-story structure of rough-sawn pine that resembled the bunkhouse of a ranch. Famous for its mesquite-broiled steaks, King Toro Steakhouse had started as a brothel sixty years ago. Its clientele had included cowboys and ranch hands as well as respectable Tucsonans, who found its distance from the city an advantage for their desert dalliance. Now it was a favorite of families, tourists, and seniors from nearby retirement communities, plus younger, harder-drinking types, who kept it filled and raucous until 3 a.m.

But at ten minutes before six, there was no sign of anyone. A rusting Pontiac sedan and a pickup truck, whose fenders were attached with wires, sat in the dirt parking lot, looking forgotten and forlorn. Jon guessed they belonged to bar patrons from the night before, who mercifully had had another person drive them home.

Jon turned in at the entrance to the lot and drove across it to the north side where the pickup sat. As Emilio had indicated, several metal drums had been placed around the lot for trash. Also at the north end of the building was what appeared to be the restaurant's kitchen. Beyond it were two, large rectangular containers topped by folding metal lids into which the kitchen staff deposited the garbage.

Jon parked beside the pickup truck and walked quickly to the bins. He discovered they were separated by a narrow space, just wide enough for him to stand in. As he'd hoped, it gave him an unobstructed view of the lot, including the trash barrel at the other end.

He reached into his pocket and took out a small, collapsible sighting scope he sometimes used for watching birds. He put it to his eye, adjusting the focus, until the words on the side of the barrel—Pitch It Here, Pardner!—were sharp and clear.

He waited.

From the bins, the smell of decomposing garbage wafted, growing stronger and more pungent. Jon tried breathing through his mouth and hoped the wait wouldn't be long.

Just then he heard the sound of an approaching vehicle.

Aiming the scope in the direction of the access road, he saw a blue Thunderbird coming at great speed. It slowed abruptly and swung into the lot, going directly to the barrel at the far end. The driver stepped out and looked around. He was an Indian, grossly overweight and wearing jeans and a white T-shirt. Leaving the engine of the Thunderbird running, he walked to the barrel and tipped it on its side. Kneeling, he pawed quickly at the earth. A moment later, Jon saw he was examining a small black object wrapped in silver tape.

The man placed the barrel upright, positioning it above the spot where he had dug. He tossed the package onto the front seat of the car and climbed in behind the wheel.

The Thunderbird made a sharp U-turn, throwing dust into the air, and accelerated from the lot.

Jon stepped out from between the bins. He took a long, deep breath, folded the spotting scope, and went immediately to his car.

ENTERING SOUTH TUCSON, the Thunderbird kept to the interstate, skirting the west side of the city. Jon stayed behind it at a distance, but still close enough to keep the car in sight.

Already the day was hot. The sky had the bleached quality of an overexposed photograph. In the summer, residents went about their lives in spite of it. But glancing toward the city as he drove, the merciless heat appeared to press down on the landscape like an iron. Except for a few high-rise buildings in the downtown area, most were of one story. Even then the vegetation remained low, with the exception of some random palms, as if reaching toward the sun would assure death.

At the sign for Grant Road, the Thunderbird abruptly braked and headed down the exit ramp. It continued east on Grant, past Oracle and Stone, before turning north again for several blocks. Finally, it drove into a used car lot that advertised itself as Monte Grande Auto Sales. On wires stretched above the sixty or so cars parked in the lot, red, yellow, and blue pennants dangled listlessly.

Jon looked for a place to park. He noticed one across the street, in front of a yellow panel truck, and eased into the space.

The Thunderbird had stopped behind a vintage Chevrolet Impala near a rear corner of the lot. The vehicle had once been white, but years of desert sun had darkened it to a dull cream. But what made it different from the rest was that it sat with its trunk facing out, and there was no suggestion of a sale price painted on the windows.

The driver left the Thunderbird and walked to the Impala, carrying the black plastic package wrapped in silver tape. He opened the trunk of the Impala with a key, tossed in the package, looked around, and closed the top. Then he returned to the Thunderbird and drove out of the lot.

Jon checked his watch. It was seven twenty-five. Traffic was already heavy on the street, and the McDonald's at the intersection near to where he'd parked was full of customers.

He was considering a quick take-out breakfast for himself, when he saw a man come through the front doors of McDonald's. The man walked quickly to the curb and, in spite of traffic, sprinted across to the car lot. From the brief look Jon had, he was in his thirties, a light-skinned Hispanic with wavy hair to which a liberal amount of pomade had been applied.

The man went directly to small white building made of cinder block that Jon guessed was the sales office. He unlocked the door and went inside. If he was the car salesman, Jon decided he would be the man's first customer.

Jon left his car where it was parked, walked to the corner, and crossed the street. He doubled back and headed to the lot. As he walked through the open gates, he could see the man was at a desk, a telephone cradled in his hand.

Jon entered the office. The man looked up at once and replaced the phone.

"The gates were open," Jon said. "I assume you're doing business."

"Ah, yes—of course." The look of surprise on the man's face gave way to the salesman's veneer. He stood and shook Jon's hand. Grasping it, Jon noticed there was a gold ring on the little finger with something affixed to it.

"Please have a seat," the man said. He waved Jon to a chair opposite the desk.

"I didn't expect to find anybody here at seven-thirty," Jon said.

"Usually there's no one. But sometimes I arrive early to catch up on paperwork."

"Are you the manager?"

"My cousin is. I help him now and then. Are you looking for a car?"

"I haven't decided."

"If so, we have some very reasonable buys." The man was once again the salesman. "For example, yesterday we received a late model Isuzu Trooper. Fine condition. We are prepared to offer it for—"

"Is your name Victor?"

There was a brief intake of breath. "No. My name is Eduardo," the man said. "Eduardo Cruz."

"Then I was misinformed. I was told that Victor would help arrange passage into the United States for certain friends of mine. Mexican friends."

"Who told you this?" The eyes narrowed, scrutinizing Jon.

"It doesn't matter," Jon said. "What matters is whether you—or Victor—can help me. If not, I'll find someone who can."

"What's your name?"

"That doesn't matter either. Did I come to the right place or not?"

This time the man said nothing. But his expression seemed to ask: Why would an Anglo with an eastern accent want to smuggle Mexicans into the United States? Jon had already prepared an answer.

"I moved to Arizona from Connecticut two years ago and bought a small ranch north of Willcox. My foreman was a Mexican. In March he went home to visit his family in Oaxaca, got into a fight, and killed a man."

"Was he arrested?"

"No. His friends hid him from the *judiciales*. The fact is I need him on my ranch to manage things. So can you help me?"

The man considered it, then shook his head. "I'm sorry. But as you yourself suggested, you have been misinformed about the nature of our business here. This is an auto dealership."

"Then I'd like to buy a car."

The look of confusion on the man's face gave way to uneasy acquiescence. He stood. "In that case, I can help. I mentioned the Isuzu. Depending on how much you're prepared to pay, we also have a good buy on a Cadillac."

"There's a white car in the lot I'd like to look at."

"Can you be more specific?" the man said. "There are several."

"It's a Chevrolet Impala. Old, with no price on the windshield."

The man shook his head. "Perhaps you're thinking of the off-white Oldsmobile. It's got sixty thousand miles but runs well enough."

"It's that car," Jon said, pointing through the window to the Impala at the rear of the lot.

The man shook his head a second time. "That car is not for sale. Frankly, I'd be embarrassed if it were. It's worth almost nothing."

"It's worth more than it was an hour ago," Jon said. "Considering what's in the trunk."

He also stood and leaned across the desk. "Look, I want three people brought over the border: my foreman; his brother, who also works at the ranch; and the brother's wife. I'm told your price is twelve hundred dollars each. I'll add a bonus of five hundred dollars, once I know they're safely here."

Again, the eyes grew small. "I finish work at three," the man said. "We can meet after that. Are you familiar with the Desert Museum?"

"Yes."

"Then you know the aviary where visitors can walk. With all the birds, it's very noisy. We can discuss matters without being overheard. Is four o'clock acceptable?"

"That's fine."

"Bring the money in large bills inside a briefcase."

"How soon after I pay you can I expect the people to arrive?" Jon asked him.

"That depends."

"On what?"

"A variety of factors," the man said. "Putting the pieces into place sometimes takes longer than we think. The people have to be contacted. They must understand the difficulties that they face. And you must understand them, too. What we are conducting is a high-risk shipping operation, nothing more."

"You make it sound as if you were transporting pottery instead of people."

The other shrugged. "The nature of the cargo isn't my concern."

"And if they die along the way?"

"As with pottery, some breakage is inevitable." The man paused. "This afternoon at four. Unless, of course, you have decided to withdraw your order."

"I'll be there."

ITS OFFICIAL NAME WAS the Arizona-Sonora Desert Museum. Spreading over twenty-one acres of high desert west of the city, it was the most popular tourist stop in Arizona after the Grand Canyon. Part zoo, part re-created habitat, it was home to hundreds of desert animals—from butterflies and bees to bears and mountain goats—in natural surroundings.

Sitting in his car near the main entrance, Jon watched people come and go. After leaving Monte Grande Auto Sales that morning, he returned to Santa Rita. From a shop that sold leather goods, he bought a cheap briefcase. Then, at the bank across the street, he arranged a money transfer from his Connecticut bank and received in return $3,600 in hundred-dollar bills.

He left his car, carrying the briefcase, and walked to the entrance. At a circular enclosure opposite two overweight iguanas dozed languidly on the hot sand. Jon purchased a ticket and headed off along a winding path.

The aviary was quite large and surrounded on all sides by thin, transparent mesh that let in air and light. Within it, visitors could stroll among native vegetation, while birds flew about or sang and chattered in the trees.

Jon sat down on a wooden bench and placed the briefcase at his feet. It was exactly four o'clock. Victor was nowhere to be seen. Still, there were about a dozen people in the aviary: couples, several families with small children, and an elderly man in a wheelchair guided by a nurse.

He also noticed a woman standing on a nearby path.

She was facing an acacia tree and appeared to be taking pictures of a Gambel's quail. She was dressed in a white blouse and a flowered skirt, with her dark hair was cut short. A large leather purse, open at the top, hung from a shoulder strap.

Although he couldn't see her face, he sensed that he had seen her somewhere recently, maybe on a field trip he'd taken with the Santa Rita birding group. Then he remembered the young Hispanic woman he'd seen in the church the day before.

"Excuse me for being late," a voice said.

Jon looked up. It was Victor.

Victor displayed a small paper bag. "I stopped to buy birdseed for my aviary friends. Feeding the birds is not allowed, of course. But when no one is looking, I scatter it."

He sat on the bench, putting the bag beside him. "How much do you know about birds?" he asked, turning.

"Not much," Jon said.

"Fascinating creatures," Victor went on in a knowledgeable tone. "Take the bird we call the night-hawk. It's not a hawk at all. And it relies on camouflage to hide its true identity. It pretends to be something it is not."

"Let's get to our business," Jon said.

Victor nodded. "Yes, of course. You have the money?"

Jon pointed to the briefcase. "Would you like to see it?"

"Yes. But not here," Victor told him. "There are people."

"My car is in the parking lot," Jon said. "We can make the transfer there."

Victor rose. "I suggest we go to my car. Maybe take a drive."

Jon picked up the briefcase and stood facing him. "It sounds like you don't trust me."

"I trust no one." Victor went on. "You are a rancher, yes?"

"That's right."

"Let me see your hands."

Jon hesitated. "What's that got to do with—"

"Show me the palms of your hands."

He grasped Jon's right hand in his own, turned it palm-side up, and studied it. Then he let it drop.

"Besides your foreman and his brother," Victor said, "you must have many people helping you. Ranching is hard work. The hands grow callous. Your hands are callused, but they are not a rancher's hands."

"I told you I was new to ranching," Jon said.

"Give me the briefcase," Victor told him.

"But I thought—"

"Give me the briefcase," Victor repeated, keeping his voice low. "Then turn around and walk slowly to the exit. I will be behind you." He put his hand into the paper bag and lifted it. "Now go."

Jon did as he was told. He gave over the briefcase, turned, and started walking toward the exit door. Directly in their path, the man in the wheelchair and his nurse had halted, while he took some pills.

Victor swore quietly. "Go around them," he ordered Jon.

"*¡Hola, Carlos!*"

Surprised, Victor turned.

It was the young woman in the flowered skirt. She touched his right arm and smiled up at him. In Spanish, she seemed to be asking him if he remembered her. Victor appeared baffled.

"*Me llamo Eduardo,*" he told her. "I'm not Carlos."

Her fingers tightened on his arm. "Remember what you told me at the party? In the bedroom?"

Victor's bafflement had turned to anger. "I'm not Carlos! Leave me alone!"

She laughed. "Naughty Carlos."

Victor dropped the briefcase and swung the paper bag around, his hand still in it. As he did, she grabbed his wrist and flung it upward, knocking the bag to the ground.

Countering, Victor propelled Jon against her. Caught off balance, Jon and the woman fell.

Victor snatched the briefcase, vaulted past the old man in the wheelchair, and plunged through the exit door.

Jon sat up. The young woman was already on her feet, talking rapidly into a cell phone. In the aviary, visitors scurried toward the exit door, ignoring the old man and the nurse, who appeared dazed.

The woman dropped her cell phone in her purse and

knelt in front of Jon. "Sorry to break up your little party, Mr. Wilder. But I probably saved your life."

She reached into her purse again, then brought up a black leather case with a gold shield and held it to his face. "Agent Montoya—U.S. Border Patrol," she said. "You and I are going to have a talk."

SIX

THEIR TALK WAS more like an interrogation. At least, it felt that way to Jon. They sat at a table in the outdoor snack bar of the museum, nestled under cottonwood trees. Both had tall glasses of iced tea in front of them. Jon occasionally sipped at his to wet his mouth. Agent Montoya ignored hers. Instead she asked questions, making notes of Jon's responses on a pad.

Jon studied her as she wrote. She was not conventionally beautiful. The face was long, the features delicate. But it was her dark eyes that held him; they were very large and soulful, yet filled with the vitality of life.

A moment after Victor fled the aviary, she'd used her cell phone to call museum security in the slim hope he could be apprehended before he left the grounds. Immediately after that, she'd called Border Patrol headquarters in Tucson and spoken with Van Dine. A half hour later, Martinez, the junior agent who had accompanied Van Dine to the old mission, arrived at the aviary. Under her direction, he collected the paper bag Victor had brought with him. Then, moving slowly on his hands and knees, he began to search the ground for evidence. Watching, Jon was reminded of a nearsighted child on an Easter egg hunt. From her disdainful glances, it was obvious Montoya had little faith in his investigative skills. Finding nothing, he'd showed the contents of the paper bag to her and left the aviary carrying it. When he was gone, she and Jon had headed to the snack bar.

"Okay," she said, finally stirring her iced tea. "Your full name is...?"

"Jonathan McNicol Wilder."

"Present address."

"I'm renting a house in Mariposa Canyon. The rest of the year I live in Scarborough, Connecticut."

She wrote down the information. "And you're an ornithologist and artist. That I know."

She folded her pad and put away her pen. "So how's your Spanish, Mr. Wilder?"

"Passable," he answered.

"Passable?"

"I had a year of it in high school. And I've picked up some since I've been here."

"Do you know the word *joder?*"

Jon shook his head.

"Politely put, it's a verb meaning 'to screw up.' Which is exactly what you did to my investigation."

"I'm sorry."

"You ought to be," she said. "Your attempt to play detective cost me months of work building a case against Ortiz."

"Ortiz?"

"Manuel Ortiz is our friend's real name. But Victor

is the alias he uses with the smugglers, so we use it, too. He's had a lot of others names and cover jobs. Last year he was a karaoke singer in a Latino nightclub, going by the name of Chico. When he sold shoes in a men's store in South Tucson, he was Tómas Salazar. When he started posing as a used car salesman, he became Eduardo Cruz.''

She added, ''As you know from visiting the lot today.''

''You saw me?''

''Remember the yellow panel truck behind you on the street outside McDonald's? For a week, we've used it for surveillance of the lot. We also planted a bug underneath the office desk. The man actually had a knack for selling cars. I might have bought one from him myself, if I didn't know his real line of work.''

''Then you heard him setting up the meeting in the aviary with me,'' Jon said.

''I did. And I knew you didn't have a clue of what you were walking into.''

''You said this is your investigation.''

''With Van Dine's blessing, yes,'' she said. ''He's my superior.''

Jon looked at her. ''You were also at the church in Santa Rita yesterday.''

''Hoping, possibly, that I could spot some guilty parties. And checking out one person who's too innocent for his own good.''

''Me?''

''You,'' she agreed. ''The first time Van Dine met you he had a feeling you'd get involved for your friend's sake. And that you'd put yourself in harm's way. Which you did.'' She paused to make sure he got the message. ''May I ask you another question?''

''Go ahead.''

''When you came here to meet with Victor, what did you believe would happen? That he'd take the briefcase with the money, tell you *gracias,* and leave?''

''I guess I did, yes,'' Jon said. ''But I'd done something to the briefcase.''

''What do you mean by 'something'?''

''I'd put a tiny homing device inside the lining of the case. Ornithologists attach them to birds' legs to study patterns of migration. The signal can be traced for miles. After Victor had gone off with the case, I planned to call Van Dine and tell him what I'd done.''

''So we'd track Victor to his nest, as if he were a bird.''

''Well, yes.''

''The fact is, Victor almost certainly took the money from the case the minute he left here,'' she answered bluntly. ''We'll probably find the briefcase, empty but still beeping, somewhere near the museum exit road.''

She took a deep drink of her iced tea and studied him over the rim of her glass. ''Now, would you like to know what would have happened to you if you'd gone with him?''

''I think I know.''

''You would have ended your days somewhere in the desert with a bullet in your brain. As for your body, you'd be a feast for desert wolves, kit foxes, bobcats, javelinas, and, of course, the vultures.''

She waited for the image to sink in. ''One final question. Why *did* you get involved?''

''To help a friend. Van Dine was right about that part of it,'' Jon said. ''Maybe I have an overdeveloped sense of justice. But after what happened to Emilio's sister and the others, I wanted to do something.'' He paused and looked at her. ''Maybe it was also because the children. I had a daughter of my own. She died when she was two. That was sixteen years ago.''

''Are you married?''

''No. My wife and daughter were killed in a car accident.''

''I'm sorry. I didn't know.'' She reached across and touched his hand. The gesture surprised him. ''It's tough when you lose someone close to you,'' she said. ''Were you also in the accident?''

''Yes. I was seriously injured. At the time, I'd been a portrait painter. But in the months it took me to recuperate, I started painting birds. Watching them gave me a sense of peace. As well as hope that over time I wouldn't feel guilty.''

''Guilty for what?''

''That of the three of us inside the car that night—''

''You lived and they didn't?''

''Yes.''

Agent Montoya nodded. ''I understand those feelings, too. But why hasn't some attractive widow or divorcée snapped you up?''

She leaned back in her chair. ''Or is it because

you're a wanderer, a roamer like the birds you follow? Lots of women want a homebody who's safely in the nest.''

"I do travel quite a bit," Jon admitted. "Maybe that's the reason."

"You're a good guy, Jon. And I don't like good guys getting hurt."

She took a breath, as if to regain her professional demeanor. "So promise me you'll get out of the amateur detective business. These smugglers are very nasty hombres. Anybody they dislike, distrust, or disagree with ends up dead. Stopping them is Van Dine's number-one priority. It's also mine. Van Dine may be a hard-ass, but he's as determined as I am to find the leader of the group. Cut off the head of the snake and the rest dies. What I don't want is other people dying needlessly. Go back to your birds and leave the dirty stuff to us."

She hoisted her bag onto the table. "I should be going. Van Dine expects a full report about this in the morning."

"Before you leave, may I ask you a question?"

"Go ahead."

"The day that Van Dine and I met, he spoke to someone on the phone. His deputy. I heard the name—"

"You heard the name Max Montoya and assumed I was a man."

He nodded.

"My full name is Maximilia," she explained. "My father was an admirer of the Mexican emperor Maximilian. If I'd been born a boy, that's the name I would have had. Max is easier. What complicates it further is that I'm not only a female agent, but also Hispanic. Hispanic officers make up forty percent of the force, and some of them are women. It also gives us an advantage when we're dealing with illegals. We speak their language, literally, and we can often get them to say things they wouldn't tell a male officer. In my case, it helps that I came here as an illegal alien myself.''

"You?''

"My father was what's known as an *indocumentado*—a person without papers. When illegals cross the Rio Grande into Texas, they're called wetbacks. Arizona and Mexico don't have a river as a border. Instead, we have a high, thick steel fence; some Mexicans call it the Tortilla Curtain. But it never stopped my father. He was a farm worker. Every year he'd make the trip from Mazatlán and travel north to Washington or Idaho; several times he even went to Florida. Sometimes he'd be caught and sent back. But he'd always try again. Then one year he was employed by a sympathetic gringo who owned a farm in Casa Grande. He saw to it that my father got an education and applied for legal status. Before the paperwork came through, my father had the rest of us brought here illegally, so we could live together as a family. He became a citizen a year before he died. In that year, he was as happy as I've ever seen.''

A museum security guard appeared along the walk.

He saw Agent Montoya, waved, and continued on his rounds.

"They're closing up," Max said. She reached into her bag and produced a small card. She scribbled on the back of it and handed it to Jon. "That's my official card, gold seal of the government and all. In case you have to contact me off hours, I've written my home number on the back."

"Thanks." Jon pocketed the card.

"And thanks for the iced tea." She stood and turned to go.

"Another question," Jon said. "But I think I know the answer."

"Ask it."

"The paper bag Victor brought with him to the aviary. Was there a gun in it?"

"Of course there was a gun." She looked at him, amused. "What were you expecting? Birdseed?"

IT WAS AFTER SEVEN when Jon turned onto the Mariposa Canyon road. The gravel road climbed steadily, with constant curves and switchbacks that veered perilously close to the mountainside. The house that Jon had rented was the last one on the road. Just beyond the gravel ended and the road became a firebreak that struggled upward toward the ridge.

Jon pulled in and parked under the shaded carport. As he stepped from the car, the bushes bordering the driveway stirred. A moment later, the jackrabbit hopped out. It stopped, its gentle brown eyes staring up at him. Its large ears twitched a greeting.

Jon returned it. "*Buenas tardes,* Señor Liebre. Sorry I was late. I'll make your dinner now and bring it to the patio."

Jon continued to the rear door of the house. He entered the kitchen, took a head of lettuce from the refrigerator, and peeled off some outer leaves. He put them on a plate, along with an old carrot and some radishes. He went through the house to the patio at the front. As he slid open the glass doors, he saw the jackrabbit was already there, waiting.

"Have a good dinner, my friend," Jon told him, setting down the plate. The jackrabbit reached it in a bound.

Returning to the kitchen, Jon fixed himself a beer. The beer was Tecate, a brand popular with Mexicans. Jon had developed a taste for it since he'd been here.

He carried it into the living room, checked the answering machine beside the telephone for messages. There were none. On the far side of the room, a television set perched on a low cabinet. He sat on the sofa opposite, picked up the remote, and clicked it on.

The program was a newscast from a local Tucson station. On the screen were two men he recognized, standing before a cluster of microphones.

One was Eric Voss; the other was Antonio Salera, the man from the parade. Both were shaking hands and smiling. On the wall behind them was a black banner with the word AMIGOS in bold red, white, and green letters: the colors of the Mexican flag. Salera stepped forward and began to speak.

"It is with great pleasure," he said, "that I accept this generous contribution to our cause."

The two men reached down and together held up a giant facsimile of a bank check made out to AMIGOS. The amount was for $1 million. The signature below was that of Eric Voss.

Now Voss took his place at the microphones. "The plight of the Mexican immigrant has always been of great concern to me," he told Salera. "Whatever can be done to ease their burden I will do."

The check was handed to a young Hispanic woman at their side. The two shook hands again.

"*Gracias. Muchas gracias, Señor* Voss," Salera said.

"*De nada,*" answered Voss as cameras flashed.

Jon turned off the set, finished his beer, and went back to the kitchen. Searching for something for himself to eat, he settled on some frozen shrimp, a hunk of supermarket cheddar, and the lettuce. He defrosted the shrimp under the kitchen faucet and threw them, along with the cheese and lettuce, into a bowl. He heated a tostada in the microwave, poured himself another beer, and placed everything on a tray.

Then he saw the small, portable radio that sat to one side of the countertop. Several nights ago, he'd turned it on and found a station in Nogales that played mostly Mexican music, everything from traditional folk ballads to *ranchero* songs. He turned on the radio and heard the first strains of a serenade.

He put the radio on the tray and carried the tray

through the house to the patio. He put the tray down on a tile table and sat on the chaise longue.

The temperature had fallen some as evening had approached. Below and to the west, the desert glowed now in a golden amber hue. Soft shadows dappled the low valleys of the Sierritas.

From the radio came a *corrida*, a folk narrative, sung by a young woman in a voice laden with despair. Although it was in Spanish, Jon knew enough to understand the words.

> *Él viene para mí esta noche;*
> *Me envolverá en sus alas;*
> *Ave de muerte—*
> *Ave de muerte…*

the singer sang:

> He comes for me tonight;
> He will enfold me in his wings;
> Bird of death—
> Bird of death.

HALF CRY, half shriek, the sound ended moments after it began. Awakened suddenly, Jon turned his head and tried to focus on the bedside clock. In the dark, the numbers glowed bloodred: 3:17.

Jon lay, not moving, waiting for the sound again. It never came.

He closed his eyes and tried to reconstruct it in his mind. Other nights, he'd heard the yipping of coyotes chasing prey. But this sound had been different. Had it been an animal at all?

He swung his legs over the bed and stood. Moving slowly to the glass doors that faced the patio, he slid apart the draperies so that he could peer out through the opening.

The sliver of a moon that had been shining earlier had disappeared. The night was black. A breeze stirred the branches of the piñon pines, giving him a sudden chill.

He went to the closet, searched until he found his bathrobe, and put it on. He remembered seeing a small flashlight in the top drawer of the bureau and located it. He flicked it on, keeping the beam directed at the floor. He moved to the glass doors again, reached through the draperies, and opened them. Quietly he stepped onto the patio.

Still with the flashlight beam directed downward, he made slow, sweeping motions across the tiles, moving the light toward the far side of the patio. Except for some dry leaves and needles from the pines, everything was as it had been hours earlier. The saucer he had left for Señor Liebre was empty, but exactly where it had been placed.

Then he saw it. Near a terra cotta pot that held small succulents, there was a dark-red spot. Crossing the patio, he knelt and touched it with a fingertip. Examining his finger in the light confirmed what he had thought. It was fresh blood. More drops were visible beyond the pot. Following them with the light, he saw they formed a path leading toward the gate separating the patio and driveway. From the first day the jackrabbit had appeared, Jon had left the gate ajar to allow it access to the patio. Now the gate was closed.

Jon opened it. The drops continued down the driveway to the road and from there along the shoulder of the road. They stopped at the base of the stone walkway leading to the front door of the house.

But instead of drops of blood, the walk was smeared with it, as if the victim had been dragged along the stones in the direction of the door.

Grimly, Jon examined each stone singly until the beam of the flashlight shone on the large woven mat beneath the door.

The mat was made of hemp, rectangular in shape and decorated with a geometric pattern in a Navajo design. But no longer was the pattern visible. Stretched out across the mat lay the mutilated body of the jackrabbit. Its throat was gashed and oozing blood. But more horrific were the three deep wounds beginning at its chest and continuing along its underbelly to its loins.

SEVEN

"WHAT A NASTY WAY for poor old Jack to meet his end," Agent Montoya said, kneeling over the doormat. "What time did you say you found him?"

"About three-thirty in the morning," Jon said.

She looked up. "Have you had any sleep since?"

"Not much. After I discovered him, I turned on all the lights, locked the doors and windows, and turned on the television. There's not much worth watching at four a.m."

She returned to the body of the jackrabbit. "That's how he was when you discovered him? Stretched across the mat like that?"

"Yes. He visited me twice a day," Jon said. "He was quite tame and friendly. He'd gotten to be something of a pet."

"The wound in the neck and those long gashes on the underside," she noted. "Could another animal have made them?"

Jon shook his head. "I doubt it. There are probably mountain lions in the area, and possibly coyotes and some wild bears. But a mountain lion would have carried off anything it killed. And bears don't look for food at this altitude unless they're desperate."

"What about a bird of prey?"

"No. They don't hunt at night, except for owls and a few others. And even if the neck wound was the cause of death, raptors use their claws to grab and hold their victims, not to leave long scars like this."

"Tell me again about the cry you heard."

"I've thought about it," Jon said. "I'm convinced it was a person trying to imitate an animal."

"Any idea who?"

Jon shook his head again.

She stood. "Do you have something to put over the rabbit and the mat for now?"

"How about a cardboard box?"

"That'll do."

Jon went to the utility closet at the back of the house, found an empty box, and returned with it. Together, they placed the box upside-down over the animal and doormat, and put several large stones on top of it to keep the box in place.

"Rest in peace, Jack," she said. "You didn't deserve this kind of death."

"Will you report this to your office?"

"I'll note it in my daily log," she told him. "But unless the rabbit hopped into the U.S. illegally, the Border Patrol won't get involved. I'll call the county sheriff's office. It's their business. They'll want to take the remains for evidence."

They started down the walk to where her car, a green Toyota, was parked along the road. "What about you? I also think the sheriff's people will want to talk with you. Will you be at the house today?"

"I'll wait for them. After that, I'd just as soon be somewhere else. Whoever carved up Señor Liebre might come back and try the same on me. As you see, the house is very isolated, and if the killer knows I'm in it by myself..."

She gave a sympathetic nod.

"But I'd still like to stay around the area. Awhile anyway. I know Cottonwood Springs has a few decent motels."

"Try the Wolfshead Inn near Rio Lobo," Max suggested. "It bills itself as a resort, but a discreet one. It has a golf course, spa, riding trails, tennis courts, even a swim-up bar, if you get thirsty while you're in the pool. The security director is a former agent. He'll make sure you don't have any visitors who are unwelcome. I'll call him if you like."

"Yes. Would you?"

"First, though, I'll notify the sheriff's people and get someone up here to talk to you soon."

"I'd appreciate that, too," Jon said.

From her cell phone she made the call, mentioned Jon's name and the location of the house, explained the circumstances, and hung up. "The sheriff's office is sending several officers right now," Max said. "Would you like me to wait with you?"

"No. I'm fine," he said, not really feeling it.

"I'd like to." She gave an offhand shrug. "I mean, part of our official duty is to protect the public. Anyway, I'd rather spend twenty minutes here protecting you than in the company of Van Dine. Until he's had his second cup of coffee in the morning, he's impossible. Do you mind?''

"Not at all.''

Max leaned back against the car. "So since you're going to hang around among us, how else do you plan to spend your time?''

"I thought I'd might visit Terravita.''

"Terravita?'' Her surprise was instant. "That place isn't exactly a theme park. Nobody gets in without an invitation from Eric Voss himself.''

"I have one. After the funeral, the Floreses had some people to their house. One of them was Voss. We were introduced, he said he knew my work, and insisted that I visit Terravita, in particular to see the birds.''

"What did you say?''

"I'd think about it.''

"Think in the affirmative,'' Max said. "You could be doing me a favor if you went there.''

"I thought you wanted me out of the detective business,'' Jon reminded her.

"I'm talking about observation, not detection,'' she said. "We have reason to believe Voss is involved in the smuggling of Mexican illegals. We don't know what his role is, but we suspect he's using Terravita as a kind of way station for incoming aliens. Our problem is we have no solid evidence to prove it or to institute a search. How much do you know about Voss, by the way?''

"Not much,'' Jon said. "Just that he's an eccentric

billionaire who has two overwhelming passions—
saving the environment and the cause of Mexican
illegals.''

"Both true," Max said. "After he got into the Mexican thing, the INS began to keep a file on him. It
makes fascinating reading.''

"Oh?''

"He was born in Malmö, Sweden, and earned a
degree in ecobiology from the University of Uppsala.
He was also blessed with family money, lots of it,
from oil, timber, minerals. After the university, he was
expected to go into the business. Instead, he became
a seaman on a freighter bound for Veracruz. Once
there, he fell instantly in love with Mexico—and with
a nightclub dancer, whom he married after a night of
wild sex and raw tequila. Her chief talent, he soon
learned, was as a prostitute. The marriage ended, but
his love affair with Mexico had just begun.''

"Could he be the leader of the smugglers?" Jon
asked.

Max thought a moment. "No. At least, I doubt it
very much. He's eccentric, but he's not mean or de-
vious enough to be a master criminal.''

"So when I visit Terravita, I should look around for
anything that seems out of the ordinary.''

"Yes," she said. "And call me when you get back
to Wolfshead.''

THE ROAD SIGN for Agua Linda suddenly came into
view. Jon eased into the right lane. He glanced down
at the dashboard clock. The time was one-fifteen. Voss
was expecting him at two.

The directions to Terravita had been explicit; Voss himself had gotten on the phone when Jon had called. Jon was to take the interstate to Agua Linda, Voss had said, then drive west along the county road for seven miles. Where the road ended, there would be an arrow pointing north to a dirt road. On the arrow Jon would see two symbols. He was to follow the dirt road for two miles until he saw the huge glass domes. A half-mile farther, he would approach a chain-link fence with an electronic gate, manned by guards. Jon was to give his name. The guards would verify it and allow him to proceed.

He turned off the highway at the exit, found the country road, and headed west. As he drove, he tried to remember everything he'd read concerning Terra-vita. Voss himself had even written a slim volume titled *Terravita: Tomorrow's World—Today!* In it Voss described his achievement of re-creating the hab-itats of the entire earth inside an enormous glass and steel complex located in the Arizona desert. Spread over many acres, it would contain every ecosystem on the planet, each carefully controlled to sustain life as it was found in its own natural environment.

It was shortly before two when the county road came to an abrupt end. Then Jon saw the arrow. On it were the two symbols Voss had mentioned. One was a six-pointed asterisk; the other, a dagger. To the casual observer they resembled marks directing readers to footnotes in a text. But Jon knew they had another meaning, too. In medicine and certain sciences, the asterisk meant birth; the dagger, death.

"BIRTH AND DEATH," Eric Voss confirmed. "You're absolutely right. And one of the few people to correctly guess my use of them. But it's what Terravita represents—birth and death and rebirth—life's eternal cycle."

Jon, Voss, and two of Voss's young assistants stood in what Voss called the Life Zone of the tropical rain forest. The four were dressed in outfits that resembled lightweight space suits. With Voss leading the way, they had already visited the Life Zones of the Sahara desert, the uplands of Nepal, a subtropical savanna, the Siberian tundra, and the Great Barrier Reef. Between each zone there was an antechamber in which their suits were sterilized, so as to prevent the transfer of microorganisms from one zone to the next.

Suddenly, in the canopy of trees and interweaving vines above, a bright-colored bird shrieked and opened its enormous bill.

"So, Mr. Wilder—" Voss said, pointing up. "Let me test your vaunted reputation for identifying birds. Can you tell me what that bird is?"

"A curl-crested aracari," Jon responded. "It's a native of southern Amazonia."

"Quite so." Voss beamed with pride. "I modeled this zone after the Altá Floresta," he went on. "Specifically, between the Tapajós and Xingu rivers. And since this is a rain forest, let's have rain."

One of the aides nodded and pressed a small handheld device. Torrents of rain immediately poured down, deluging the trees and forest floor. A minute after it began, the aide activated the device again and the rain stopped.

Voss turned to Jon. "The next zone is the coastal floodplain."

The four men walked from the rain forest, through the transfer chamber, and into a scene that convinced Jon he was in the Mississippi delta. Stretching before them was a furrowed field of dark, rich earth, across which small green shoots were visible. Surrounding the field were varieties of shrubs and trees: sweet gum and redbud and live oaks draped with Spanish moss.

"Behold the Life Zone of the agricultural floodplain," Eric Voss announced. Again he addressed Jon. "I assume you know the birds that are indigenous to this environment."

"Among others," Jon said, "the Mississippi kite, the lark sparrow, and depending on sufficient water—"

"There's a lake just beyond the trees," Voss said.

"A Louisiana heron," Jon continued, "and a mottled duck."

"We'll see if you're right."

Voss started off, waving to the group to follow him. They skirted the field and pushed through a copse of southern pines. Beyond the trees was a small lake, just as Voss had said. In the shallows at the far end stood a Louisiana heron, while in the lake itself, a dozen mottled ducks were bickering for food.

"See there?" Voss called out, pointing at the topmost branches of an oak. "I also have a yellow-throated warbler."

But Jon's attention was directed at the shoreline of the lake ahead of where they stood.

"FOOTPRINTS? Are you sure?" Max asked him.

"Yes."

"How many?"

"Five," Jon said. "Plus one partly washed away by the water of the lake."

Earlier that day, Jon had told the real estate agent he was giving up the Mariposa Canyon house and checked into the Wolfshead Inn. Now, sitting on the bed in his room, he heard Max cover the phone. A muffled conversation followed. She came back on the line. "You're certain the prints were human and not animal?"

"Unless the animal wore size-ten sneakers."

"Tell me again where you were when you spotted them," she asked.

"We'd entered the section Voss call the agricultural floodplain. In it is a small lake. The trees are close to the water's edge. I learned that just outside the section is a door leading to a service hall. I'm guessing somebody came through the door, entered the trees, and stepped into the mud beside the lake before realizing his mistake."

"Voss must have other employees who use those doors," Max suggested. "Maybe it was one of them."

"I thought about that," Jon said. "But everyone working in the complex wears special suits. And the imprints the shoes leave are very different."

"Anything else?"

"Yes. After the tour, Voss walked me to my car. I'd parked it in a lot bordering a pecan grove. When I asked about the grove, he said it had been there when he bought the property. He'd kept it as it was. As we approached my car, I saw more footprints in the grove. The irrigation sprinklers had been on earlier that day, and in spots the ground was damp. That's where I saw the footprints."

"Did they also look like sneakers?"

"Sneakers, sandals, even those Mexican huaraches that use pieces of old tire tread."

"Could they have been made by field hands?" she asked.

"This isn't harvest season. And the prints were in a straight line leading toward the door Voss and I had just used."

"Did Voss notice the prints, too?"

"I don't think so."

"That's it then?" she concluded.

"One more thing," Jon said. "While I was there, Voss invited me to dinner at his house tonight. I accepted."

Max sounded pleased. "Good. Maybe you'll notice something else that doesn't seem right. Call me at home tonight."

"Sure."

"Speaking of dinner, and to repay you for your investigative work, how about something at my place tomorrow night? It won't be as sumptuous as what you'll get at Voss's place tonight, but I can still whip up a mean *pescado veracruzano*. Seven o'clock?"

"Seven is fine."

"You're on." She gave him the address of her apartment on the north side of the city. "And Jon—"

"Yes?"

"Thank you," she said. "For a lot of things."

The phone clicked off.

EIGHT

IT WAS NOT QUITE eight when Jon arrived at Eric Voss's house. The house, which Voss called La Hacienda, was a sprawling structure of cream white stucco walls and terra cotta Spanish tiles. Studying it in the twilight as he came up the winding drive, Jon thought it resembled the residence of an eighteenth-century grandee, when the colony that is now Mexico was called New Spain. Surrounding it were vast expanses of green lawns, flowering shrubs and carefully tended trees.

Jon parked his car in a broad, gravelled area in front of the house and started up the walk. As he climbed the steps to the front door, it suddenly swung open and two figures appeared: a young woman and an older man, both Hispanic. The pair, in fact, seemed out of another century. The woman wore an ankle-length black peasant skirt and a white blouse that tied in front. The man was in a loose-fitting white shirt and dark knee breeches. For a moment, Jon thought of all the Zorro movies he had seen.

"*Buenas noches,* Mr. Wilder," the man announced. "Mr. Voss has not yet returned, but he is expected momentarily. He asked that you please wait in the library.''

Once past the massive wooden door, the man escorted Jon along a tiled hall. Hung along the stucco walls were works of art that ranged from exquisite jade carvings under glass by Olmec artisans to paintings by Rivera and Tamayo.

The library itself was large with windows, a stone fireplace, and floor-to-ceiling bookshelves lining the remaining walls. In the fireplace a fire burned, fueled by mesquite and what appeared to be dried sections of saguaro cactus ribs.

"Do you desire a cocktail, perhaps, sir?" the man asked Jon.

"I'll wait till Mr. Voss is here," Jon said.

The servant bowed and left the room. On the mantelpiece above the fireplace a clock chimed eight.

While he waited, Jon studied the bookshelves. They suggested Eric Voss's wide and varied tastes. Among them were books on Norse mythology, Mayan hieroglyphic picture books called codices, a thick volume on the flora of the Iberian Peninsula, and a first-edition copy of the works of Baudelaire. Nearby, on a reading stand, was a quarto volume of original bird paintings by John James Audubon. Jon had rarely seen the complete volume outside of museums. Gingerly he began looking through the paintings, once more in awe of the genius Audubon possessed.

The mantel clock chimed eight-fifteen. Jon wondered briefly what was keeping Voss and went back to the Audubons.

Then, at a distance, he heard a man's voice, followed by footsteps in the hall. The library opened and a man entered. It was Luis Cardenal. Seeing Jon, he stopped abruptly.

"Mr. Wilder—we meet again," Cardenal said. Dressed in a black business suit, he looked especially austere. "I gather Eric isn't here."

"Not yet."

"Unlike him," Cardenal said. "The man is usually quite punctual. Have you been waiting long?"

"Twenty minutes, maybe," Jon guessed.

"I hoped to be here earlier myself. But I had business in Sonora, and the border crossing took longer than I thought."

The manservant reappeared carrying a drink in a tall glass. Cardenal took it, saying nothing. When the servant had gone, Cardenal turned again to Jon.

"Tell me if you would," he said, "how well do you know Eric Voss?"

"Not well," Jon admitted.

"For that matter, how well does anyone know Eric Voss?" the man observed. "I consider him a friend and we've been involved in several business ventures recently. But I find him an enigma." Cardenal looked around the room. "I also find much of this house and Eric's efforts to recapture colonial Mexico patronizing and insulting, especially to one who is Mexican, such as myself. Look at the way he dresses up his servants. I appreciate his interest in our culture. But this—this is mockery."

He checked his watch impatiently. "I have calls to

make. Would you excuse me if I did so from another room until Eric arrives?''

''Not at all.''

Cardenal left the library. Jon returned to the Audubons.

Eight-thirty came. Eight forty-five.

The library door suddenly swung open. Cardenal stood in the doorway. He was flushed with rage. ''I've spoken to the servants and they have no idea where he is. I'm going. What about you?''

''I'll wait a few more minutes,'' Jon said.

''Very well.'' Cardenal strode away, his footsteps sounding on the tile hall. Soon after, Jon heard the crunch of tires on the gravel drive.

At nine, Jon decided that he, too, had waited long enough. He suggested to the manservant that there must have been a mixup and to explain to Mr. Voss when he appeared. The servant, for his part, was profuse in his apologies as he escorted Jon to the front door.

Walking down the steps, Jon realized another car was parked behind his own: a white Mercedes. He guessed that it was Voss's car and started for it, expecting the man would step from it to greet him.

Jon was right about one thing: Voss was behind the wheel. But he did not step out. Instead, his head was tilted awkwardly against the headrest. The seat belt had been removed. The man's eyes and mouth were open. There was a deep wound in the center of his throat from which great amounts of blood had poured.

The white shirt Voss had worn had been ripped open, exposing the man's chest.

Starting just below the wound and running downward to his abdomen were three long scars.

THE WOLFSHEAD INN, as Max Montoya had suggested, was an attractive and discreetly private hotel resort. Its architecture was in the southwestern style, with a large central building housing shops and restaurants, and guest rooms in adjoining casitas that surrounded the inn's golf course and a small lake. Located near the town of Rio Lobo, it had a reputation for unostentatious luxury and for the anonymity that it afforded guests. It was the privacy and not the luxury that Jon sought now.

Yesterday, after leaving the Mariposa Canyon house and surrendering the keys to Billy Ketchum, Jon had checked in about four. He'd taken a short nap, then showered and dressed. At seven-thirty he had set off for Eric Voss's house for what he now thought of as the dinner invitation from hell. After reporting Voss's death to the police and giving interviews to them when they arrived, he'd gone back to the inn and called Max, telling her everything he had told them. Finally, he'd fallen into the king-size bed and slept a fitful sleep, interrupted by nightmarish dreams in which Voss's mutilated body reappeared. He'd awakened the next morning and ordered coffee in his room.

He'd hardly finished when the call came from the front desk. It was Max Montoya. Could she talk with him? she asked. Jon agreed. Five minutes later she was at his door.

"Tonight's dinner is still on, but there's something I wanted to talk with you about." She noticed he was glancing past her to a golf cart parked along the walk. "I borrowed the cart from my friend who runs security. Do you mind going for a ride?"

"Not at all."

They started down the walkway to the cart, climbed in, and headed off.

"About last night," Max said, apropos of nothing, "when we talked, you mentioned Luis Cardenal. I spoke with the sheriff's people earlier this morning. Cardenal claims there was no other car in the driveway except yours when he left the house."

"Do you think Cardenal might have been involved in Voss's death?"

"We're checking into it," she answered noncommittally. "If he was, he probably hired someone else to do the dirty deed. Cardenal seems like too classy a guy to make a bloody mess like that. Especially with you and the two servants there who could place him at the scene."

"When will you get the medical examiner's report?"

"In a few days," Max said. "That'll tell us how he died. But we still don't know why. I have my own ideas, though. For one thing, we've been hearing rumors lately that the smugglers considered Voss a liability. In spite of all the help he may have given them, he was an idealist and an eccentric. Also, a loose cannon in an otherwise clandestine operation. So he had to go.''

The path sloped down to a golf course. They began to parallel the seventh green. Looking toward it, Jon saw four golfers gesticulating over the dynamics of a downhill lie.

Max slowed the cart and turned into a small rest area flanked by desert willows. "We can talk here." She left the cart and walked to a wooden bench nearby. Jon joined her.

For some moments she was silent, watching the golfers on the fairway opposite from where they sat. "I have something to give you," she said at last. She reached into her purse and withdrew a small manila envelope.

"Take this," she told him. "I'll explain."

"What is it?"

"Open it."

Jon tore open the envelope. Inside was an audiocassette. He turned it over in his hand, hoping to see something that would identify the contents. There was nothing.

"Please listen to the tape," she said. "All I can get out of it are unintelligible noises. There are also supposed to be bird sounds."

"What sort of birds?"

"You're the expert. Maybe you can tell."

"Who recorded it?" Jon asked her.

"Another agent. This spring he was assigned to infiltrate the smugglers. He traveled undercover into Mexico, posing as a laborer, and linked up with some illegals who were being smuggled to the United States. On his own, he decided to wear a listening device. Several hours after midnight, the group crossed the border somewhere near Sasabe. Apparently, the smugglers use three locations where they drop the illegals after they've been brought in.''

''Do you know the locations?''

''Monte Dulce, Kyler's Pass, and Oro Rojo. They're all abandoned mining towns. He and the others were deposited at Kyler's Pass by the first group of *coyotes* who'd transported them on this side of the border. They were to be picked up by a second group who'd take them north. While they waited, a rumor began circulating that the leader of the smugglers himself would appear. A short time later, he said he heard the kind of call a bird would make. It was repeated several times. After them came another sound that made no sense. Then the tape ends.''

''What happened to the agent and the others?''

''Several pickup trucks arrived. He and the illegals climbed into them and were driven to a safe house south of Tucson. The next day they were free to go.''

Jon held up the cassette. ''You want me to listen to this and identify the bird the agent spoke about?''

''Or if it's a bird at all,'' Max said. ''I've played the tape a dozen times and I can't hear any bird I recognize.''

''The agent who gave you the cassette,'' Jon asked. ''Is he also stationed at the Tucson headquarters?''

''He was,'' Max said. ''He died this spring.''

''Was he a friend?''

Max looked at him. "My best friend. His name was Roberto. He was my husband."

THE TAPE WAS indecipherable; Max had been right. Using an audiocassette player he'd borrowed from the inn, Jon sat at the desk in his room, playing and replaying the tape. Nothing on it sounded like a bird he could identify.

He rewound the tape, pressed Stop, then Play. The first few minutes of the tape provided only background noises. Suddenly came three sharp squeaks in quick succession, followed by the unintelligible sounds that Max had mentioned. Soon after that the tape went dead.

Then Jon recalled a lecture he had once given to a birding group. A tape recording had been made of it, but at a speed that was too slow. When played normally, his voice sounded as if he'd been inhaling helium. This tape also could have been recorded at a slower speed, so that the bird sounds were, in fact, the high-pitched squeaks he'd heard.

Jon examined the machine. There was a dial that controlled volume and other basic operations, such as play, rewind, eject, and stop. But nowhere could the tape speed be adjusted.

Then he remembered Father Flannery. The priest had mentioned he had sound equipment that allowed him to listen to the calls of birds.

Jon phoned the concierge desk of the inn and asked if they would find for him the number of St. Anne's Church in Santa Rita.

"WE'LL GO TO my study," Father Flannery said, greeting him at the door of the rectory. He led the way along a hall and opened a door at the far end. The study was small but welcoming, with colorful weavings decorating the walls and a large Navajo rug spread out across the floor. A crucifix with a Hispanic-looking Christ gazed down from the wall over the priest's desk.

On the opposite side of the room, a reel-to-reel sound unit sat on a long table with speakers on each side and reels of tape stacked nearby. Father Flannery gestured to a chair for Jon and pulled up another for himself facing the table. He pushed the power button and the unit sprang to life.

"Give it a minute to warm up," he said. "Then I'll transfer what's on the audiocassette to a reel." He placed a blank tape on a spindle, attached the take-up reel on the other, and inserted the cassette into the tape holder.

"The sound I want to hear played back starts about four minutes into the tape," Jon suggested.

"I'll run it down a ways and start recording." The priest pressed the fast forward button for the cassette and it sped ahead. Suddenly they heard three squeaks.

"That's it," Jon said at once.

Father Flannery briefly rewound the cassette, then let it play, at the same time transferring it to a reel of tape. The moment the squeaks ended, he stopped the cassette and the reel on which the squeaks had been recorded, rewound that portion of the reel, and played it back at a slower speed.

What both heard was a shrill *pweee* sound, repeated twice and trailing off each time. There was a pause and then, faintly, what appeared to be a chicken clucking. It caught Jon by surprise.

"I didn't hear that when I played the cassette," he told the priest.

"You probably wouldn't have. It's mixed up with background noises. My guess is it's one of the *coyotes* acknowledging the other sound. It sounded like a person trying to imitate a chicken. That would make sense."

"Why?"

"Smugglers refer to the illegals as *pollos*—it's the Spanish word for chickens."

"Play the first three sounds again," Jon asked.

Father Flannery rewound the reel and replayed the sounds. Finally, he swung around. "And what bird would you say that is?" he asked.

"The broad-winged hawk. No question. It's a distinctive call."

"I'd say so, too," Father Flannery agreed. "And an excellent imitation. It's also understandable whoever runs the smugglers would choose that sound. Hawks are powerful. They're feared. They lord it over certain other birds. What better way to throw fear into those poor *pollos?*"

"Besides, it's rare to find a broad-winged hawk west of the Rocky Mountains," Jon said. "They're eastern and midwestern birds almost exclusively. I've watched hundreds migrating over the Great Lakes."

"And if its call was used as some sort of a signal,"

Father Flannery added, "it wouldn't be confused with any local bird."

The priest was pensive. "And there's one more thing about the hawk that could increase a person's fear. Since you've been in Arizona, has anyone spoken of *el halcón satánico*—the devil's hawk?"

"No. But it sounds ominous."

"It's meant to be," Father Flannery assured him. "I'm told it started as a legend centuries ago. But I still hear it now and then, particularly in this part of the Southwest and northern Mexico. The legend goes that if a person looks up and sees a great bird, black and circling above them, they will die. The bird is Satan's messenger announcing their damnation for eternity."

"Has anybody seen this so-called devil's hawk and lived?"

"A few. The antidote, apparently, is to make an immediate novena to the Virgin of Guadelupe and devote your life to Christ. I'm sure the bird they've seen is nothing but a common turkey vulture. It's mostly black, of course, except for the reddish head. But seeing the silhouette of it from far below, no one can make that distinction. And in flight, as you well know, the bird looks massive, gliding on those outstretched wings. For someone who has heard the legend and is close to death, the sight of it is enough to produce enormous terror. Even hasten death in certain instances."

The priest became reflective once again. "When I first came to Santa Rita, there was an old man living on the outskirts of the town. How old, no one knew, including him. He'd been diagnosed with cancer. It was terminal. One day I paid a pastoral visit at the family's request. It was a lovely day in late October. I arrived at his son's house where he was staying and found the old man outside on a shaded patio. We spoke awhile, he and I. We prayed together. When we were done, he took my hand and thanked me in Spanish—he spoke no English. Suddenly he pointed to the sky. *'El halcón satánico,'* he whispered to himself. I still had my sight then. I looked up and saw the bird. It was very high and seemed to float on air, its outline etched against the sun.

"*'El halcón satánico,'* the old man said a second time. And then he died."

NINE

LIKE MUCH OF America, Tucson had been extensively malled, most of the malls so similar they seemed to have been produced by template. St. Philip's Plaza, on the other hand, was an exception: an attractive, moderate-size complex with a hotel, restaurants, shops, and winding, tree-lined streets. Jon had a dislike of shopping malls in general. But Max had mentioned it during their phone call of the night before.

He'd called to tell her what he and Father Flannery had learned from the cassette. During their conversation, she'd reaffirmed her dinner invitation for tonight, and Jon had offered to bring wine. He'd also asked if she knew of a good wine shop in the city. She'd suggested something called Great Spirits in St. Philip's Plaza. He'd made a note of it.

Jon left the Wolfshead Inn soon after lunch and drove to the city. He went, first, to the Tucson Audubon Society headquarters near the campus of the university. Hoping to buy a copy of his own nature guide to Mexican birds, he'd learned they'd sold the last in stock that day. He left the building after four. With three hours of free time before Max expected him, he decided to pick up the wine, then visit an art dealer on the north side of the city who'd been interested in purchasing his work.

From the Audubon headquarters, he drove north on Campbell, crossed the dusty wash that was the Rillito River, and turned into the plaza entrance. As he slowed at the pedestrian crosswalk, he heard tires squealing to a stop.

Looking in the mirror, he saw a cream Jaguar sedan with tinted windows, apparently impatient to turn in as well. Jon drove around until he found the wine shop. He pulled into a parking space and went inside. From the proprietor, he bought a pleasant pinot blanc and had the bottle gift-wrapped.

As Jon left the shop and walked in the direction of his car, he saw the Jaguar was now parked in the space adjacent to it. Jon was approaching his car when two men stepped out of the Jaguar, leaving the doors open. Both men were Hispanic, short and muscular. In their dark business suits, white shirts, and ties they looked like well-dressed fireplugs. Momentarily, Jon wondered why anyone would choose to wear such outfits in this heat. One of the men came toward him.

"*Señor* Wilder," the man said, making the name sound like "Wielder."

Jon stopped, surprised. "That's right."

"Please come with us," the other man announced, stepping between Jon and his car.

"Who are you?"

"We have an invitation to extend to you," the first man said somewhat awkwardly.

"An invitation from whom?"

"Our employer would like you to accompany us to his home."

"Well, tell your employer my dance card is filled," Jon said. The men stared blankly. "I have dinner plans. ¿Comprende?"

The men nodded.

"Now, please excuse me." Jon reached for the door handle of his car.

As he did, one grabbed his arm; the other put a bear hug on him from behind and began pulling him toward an open door of the Jaguar. With his free hand, Jon swung the bottle at the man in front of him, and missed. The man wrenched the bottle away. It flew up into the air and landed on the pavement, smashing into bits.

Hands pinned behind him now, Jon was shoved into the rear seat of the Jaguar. One man jumped in beside him, the other in the front.

A moment later, the Jaguar sped out of the plaza, heading north.

"MY APOLOGIES for the way in which my men persuaded you to visit me," Antonio Salera said. "They're new members of my staff."

"You mean they haven't finished goon school?" Jon asked the man.

Salera smiled, ignoring the remark. They were seated on the veranda of Salera's house, bordered by eucalyptus, paloverde, and acacia trees and red and purple bougainvillea. The house, set high in the mountains north of Tucson, was mostly glass, the walls jutting forward at dramatic angles to take full advantage of the view.

"Cigar?" Salera asked. He pointed to a polished teakwood humidor that sat on a low table.

"I don't smoke."

"Neither should I," Salera said. "My doctor's always telling me it's not in my best interest." He gave a laugh. "But all my life people been telling me what's in my best interest, and they've usually been wrong."

Salera took a cigar from the humidor and lit it. As he took a long, deep draw, Jon studied him. The man was older than Jon remembered from the parade some weeks ago in Santa Rita. But the magnetism was the same. He was again dressed in a flowered shirt and dungarees, but unlike those he wore in the parade, these were by Ralph Lauren. The sandals were from Kenneth Cole. The massive wooden chair in which he sat resembled the throne of a conquistador.

"You'll agree," the man went on, "that Eric Voss's death was a great tragedy. He was a friend, you know."

"I know he was a benefactor of AMIGOS," Jon acknowledged.

"Yes. He will be missed."

From the offhand way Salera said it, Jon wasn't sure if it was Voss or Voss's money that would be missed more.

"I also know," Salera said, "that you were to have dined with him the night he died."

"How do you know that?"

"I saw Voss earlier that day. He mentioned it." Salera took another draw on his cigar, the smoke drifting upward languidly in the still air. "In fact, I know many things about you, Mr. Wilder. How much do you know about me?"

"I know you were important in the labor movement in the sixties," Jon said.

"Yes," Salera said. "I started as a worker in the pecan groves and went on to found a union. What César Chavez did for grapes, I did for nuts. Our strike of the farm workers who picked nuts did far more to hurt the American economy than most people were aware." Salera smiled. "Some government officials admitted privately that my union and I had Uncle Sam by the nuts."

A maid appeared and Salera spoke to her in Spanish. He glanced over at Jon. "Would you care for some *agua mineral*—mineral water?" he asked. "It's very refreshing on a day as warm as this. Of course, you're welcome to have anything you like."

"I'd like a good bottle of pinot blanc to replace the one I lost."

"I apologize again for the behavior of my men. You'll be given a replacement, certainly."

He dismissed the maid and waved a hand in the direction of the city that stretched out far below. "Since you arrived, I hope you've had the opportunity to appreciate the view. It's quite extraordinary, don't you think?"

"I also thought it was federally protected forest land," Jon told him.

"Except for my five hundred acres, yes." Salera said. "Centuries ago, it was given over as a Spanish land grant when this region was a portion of New Spain. For reasons too complicated to explain, it came into my possession. The government has been fighting in the courts for years to get it back. Unsuccessfully, I'm glad to say. So here we sit. Do you know the motto of the state of Arizona, by the way?"

Jon shook his head.

"*Ditat Deus*. God enriches. Arizona—and the United States—have been exceptionally good to me since I first came here from Oaxaca with no money and no hope."

Jon leaned forward. "Look, you didn't have me kidnapped and brought here to talk about your rags-to-riches story. What is it you want?"

Salera pointed to a bell-shaped bird feeder hanging from a nearby paloverde tree. Hovering around it were two hummingbirds. The male, Jon could see, had a glittering green underside and wings, and a tail that was a deep, rich red.

"I'm sure you recognize the Berylline hummingbirds," Salera said.

"I saw them several years ago in Mexico," Jon said. "Their color is remarkable."

"Each day they come here at this time to feed," the man went on. "But as you point out, they are not native to this area. They are strays, what ornithologists call 'accidentals'—'vagrants.' Put another way, they're undocumented aliens. Still, they're more fortunate than many of their human counterparts. They cross the border when and where they choose. They're not required to show papers providing their identity, nor asked demeaning questions by authorities, nor subjected to humiliating body searches, which, for the women, may be at the hands of leering border guards.''

Salera paused. "I'm sure that you're concerned, yes, angered, to see birds abused. Mistreated. Left to die.''

"Of course.''

"Just as I am when I observe the treatment of my countrymen,'' Salera said. "I've been luckier than most. And still I suffer for them just the same. Now I have the opportunity to help them.''

"Through AMIGOS?''

"That's one way among, certainly. The border that runs from the Pacific Ocean to the Gulf of Mexico joins two great countries, Mexico and the U.S. But it separates them, too. Every day hundreds come to the United States to seek a better life. And when the laws prohibit them from doing that, they will find illegal means through smugglers.''

Salera ground what was left of his cigar into an ashtray. When he looked up again, his face was hard. "So let this come as a suggestion and a warning, Mr. Wilder. Cease your efforts to learn more about the men who are behind the smuggling of Mr. Flores's sister and the rest.''

"I'm not conducting the investigation,'' Jon told him. "The Border Patrol is.''

"Please. I'm not naive. I know you're aiding them.

I also know that their investigation may have some success. But the leader of the syndicate, the one who guides and motivates them, he will not be caught. He is a clever man.''

''Do you know who the leader is?'' Jon asked.

''I didn't say that.''

''Do you?''

The man hesitated. ''I have my suspicions, yes.''

''Then why not share them with the authorities,'' Jon said, ''and end the mistreatment of the illegals who you care about?''

''Because it won't. Attempts to name their leader and expose their operation are a futile exercise. It would only make the man himself more dangerous, and as a result, more of the innocent will die.''

Salera let the thought hang in the air, then added, ''Even you.''

He looked past Jon. ''Ah—*bueno*. My men are waiting to return you to the city and your car.''

Salera stood. At the far end of the path he saw the two dark-suited thugs who had abducted him. Both smiled diffidently.

''*Por favor, Señor Wielder,* to come with us,'' one of the men said.

The other held up what appeared to be a bottle, also gift-wrapped.

''Thank you for granting us the time to talk,'' Salera said. ''I hope you understand the meaning of my words.''

Jon also stood and faced him. ''They were hardly subtle.''

''I am not a subtle man,'' Salera said.

MAX TOOK the wrapping from the bottle of champagne, "Cristal—1985," she said, examining the label. "You really know how to impress a girl. I was expecting wine."

"You almost had wine," Jon said, stepping into her apartment. "It's a long story."

"Good. I like stories. But I like champagne even better. Shall we have it now or save it for dinner?"

"Whatever you like."

"I vote for now. You pour while I start fixing things." She closed the door and started toward the kitchen, carrying the bottle.

The apartment was bright and cheerful with a hallway leading off to other rooms. Beyond the living room was a small dining area, open to the kitchen and separated from it by a serving shelf.

Max led him into the kitchen. From a cabinet, she took two champagne glasses and put them on the countertop. She handed Jon the bottle. "Now your work begins."

He began peeling off the wire coif. As he did, he saw an empty bubble gum wrapper lying in the sink. He picked it up. "This yours?" he asked.

Max snatched it from his hand. "Bubble gum is a secret vice of mine." She tossed the wrapper in the trash.

"What others do you have?"

"If I told you, they wouldn't be secret, would they? But with enough champagne, you might discover some." She smiled. "Consider yourself warned. So pour."

Jon filled the two glasses. Max raised hers and touched it to his. "*Salud.* Now tell me the story, while I work."

She took an avocado from a bowl, removed the skin and the pit, and began slicing the avocado into pieces. As she did, Jon told about her the encounter with Salera. Max listened, nodding several times. "At least you got an expensive bottle of champagne out of it," was all she said.

She tossed the pieces of avocado in the blender and pushed the button. "Well, I have two pieces of information that should interest you," she said.

"This morning I checked into how Eric Voss had been spending his time lately. A month ago, he bought a great deal of property a few miles from the Mexican border. Looking at it, all you see is empty desert. Below the surface, though, it's catacombed with tunnels. They were originally dug by mining companies operating in the area. Some tunnels even have the old narrow tracks the ore cars used."

"You think Voss bought the land so he could use the tunnels for transporting illegal aliens?"

"That's my guess," Max said. "But there's more to it than that. Voss could have financed the transaction out of his own pocket. But instead, he borrowed money from a bank. Luis Cardenal's bank."

She pushed a button on the blender, watching as the blades turned the avocado sections to green pulp.

"You said there were two pieces of information," Jon reminded her.

"Yes." She turned to him and smiled. "First, I'll have some more champagne."

Jon refilled her glass. She touched it to his, said *Salud* a second time, and took a sip. "When you told me last night that the sound on the cassette was probably a hawk, it reminded me of something. So today I searched through a packet of old files and came across an incident that was investigated by the Yuma sector several years ago. Two illegals were murdered in a very gruesome way. Both men had worked as gardeners, and when they entered the U.S. they brought along the tools of their trade.

"According to an illegal who witnessed it, they had a disagreement of some sort with the smugglers and were stabbed to death with their own pruning shears. But for the leader of the smugglers that wasn't enough. After they were dead, he disfigured their bodies with one of those little handheld gardening rakes, leaving deep scars down their chests and abdomens. The agents said it was the most sadistic thing they'd ever seen. It was as if the two had been the victims of some giant bird. As a result, the leader of the smugglers who'd killed them was nicknamed The Hawk. It must have gotten back to him, because a month later another poor illegal was murdered the same way. But this time, there was a stab wound to the neck as well as the three scars on the chest."

"The same as the wounds on the jackrabbit," Jon said.

"Yes. And those on Eric Voss. By the way, I called a friend in the medical examiner's office the day we found the jackrabbit at your door. He had the sheriff's department send the carcass to him for a forensic check. He told me there were some carpet fibers in the rabbit's wounds, probably from the weapon that the killer used. I'm sure they'll find the same fibers in the wounds on Voss."

"Could he confirm where they came from?" Jon asked.

"He'll know in a few days and send a full report."

Max stopped the blender. "But enough of this fun talk. Let's get on with dinner."

She poured the avocado paste into a mixing bowl and began adding pieces of red chili. "By the way, I changed my mind about *pescado*. What I'm doing is a special family recipe, plus what I've picked up on my own."

The meal, as Max promised, was a combination of Mexican and southwestern specialties—gazpacho, quesadillas, and a green salad—*ensalada de lechuga*, she translated, to begin. For the entree, she served *enchilada de crema con guacamole*. By the end of dinner, the last of the champagne had been consumed.

"How have you been doing with your Spanish?" she asked him, as she cleared the table.

"All right, I guess. I manage."

"Then you deserve a lesson tonight. We'll begin with *café y postre* in the living room."

"*Café* is coffee, I know," Jon said. "But *postre*—"

"Dessert. *Pastelito de fruta*."

"My high school Spanish lessons never got me to dessert," Jon said. "We stopped with *burritos*."

"Then we'll make tonight's lesson intensive." She drained the last drops of her champagne and disappeared with the glass into the kitchen.

Moving to the living room, Jon took the opportunity to look around a second time. There was a small fireplace at one end of the room that he hadn't noticed earlier. Framed photographs were set along the mantel. Among them was an assortment of what looked like family pictures, including a group of children at play. There was also a photo of a younger Max with her arm around a handsome, athletically built Hispanic man. Jon guessed the man was Max's husband.

As he was studying it, she returned from the kitchen, carrying a tray.

He gestured to the photograph. "You and Roberto?"

"Yes. It was taken on our honeymoon." She set down the tray on the coffee table by the sofa. On it were cups and saucers, a carafe, and a plate of pastries, as well as a bottle of cognac and two glasses. Max seated herself and began pouring coffee into the cups.

Jon joined her. "Were you and he the only ones to listen to the undercover tape Roberto made?"

She nodded. "Yes."

"What happened then?"

Max added sugar to her coffee, saying nothing as she stirred the cup. "After Roberto and the others were released from the safe house, he made his way back here. He was due to return to duty the next day. That morning, I watched him from the window as he left the building. He was walking toward the parking lot when another car pulled up. Someone called his name. He turned. Shots were fired and the car took off. I screamed. I ran downstairs to where he lay. He was already dead.''

"And the cassette?'' Jon asked.

"He'd left it with me.'' She looked at Jon. "He said never to tell anyone about it, except somebody I trusted totally.''

"Thank you,'' Jon said simply. "But was there a reason why he didn't give it to his superiors.''

"He said the listening device had been his own idea, not theirs, and they might not have approved. I think there was another reason, too.''

"Which was?''

"He suspected someone at Border Patrol headquarters might be an informant for the smugglers. He didn't want to take that risk.''

She offered him the plate of pastries. "Here, have some *pastelitos,*'' she said, changing the subject. "Now tell me more about your life. I know your wife and daughter died. Did you ever remarry?''

"No.''

"You also said you live in Scarborough, Connecticut. Where's that?''

"Along the water in the southeast corner of the state.''

"Sounds nice,'' Max remarked. "And what sort of a house is it? I'm guessing very modern, lots of glass, with water views.''

"You're right about the water views. Otherwise, it's a big fieldstone monstrosity with turrets at each end. My friends call it the Castle."

"Where you reside in royal splendor like a king."

"Not quite."

"At least, the solitary genius then."

"Not quite to that, either," Jon said.

"Then there's someone in your life."

"Yes."

"Name of?" Max inquired.

"Lorelei. She has an antiques shop in town. We met several years ago, when she moved to Scarborough to get over a nasty divorce. We became friends."

"Good friends I take it."

"Yes."

"Have you ever done a portrait of her?"

"No. After I began painting birds, I gave up portrait painting altogether. Maybe I'm more fond of birds than people," he admitted.

"Which reminds me," Max said. She rose and left the room, returning several moments later, carrying a book. She held it up. "*Wilder's Birds of Mexico.* My luck, it was the last copy they had at the Tucson Audubon Society."

"I tried to buy one this afternoon and they told me they were out of stock."

"Would you mind signing it?" she asked. "I want to give it as a gift."

"Certainly." He took a pen from an inner pocket of his jacket. "How should I make it out?"

"For Bobito," Max told him.

"Bobito?"

"He's a relative."

"Is he a birder?"

"He loves birds."

Jon inscribed the book, signed it "Cordially, Jon Wilder," and returned it to her.

"Thank you," she said. "He'll like that."

She sat again on the sofa, this time taking off her shoes and tucking her feet under her. She flipped through the pages of the book. "After I bought it, I skimmed it to see if you gave any of the birds their Spanish names. Except for the Aztec thrush, all of them sound Anglo—the yellow grosbeak, the streaked-back oriole, the crescent-chested warbler."

"There's a Spanish-language version of the guide," Jon said. "But I left the names to a translator."

"Then you need a Spanish lesson, definitely," she assured him. She lifted the bottle of cognac. "We'll start with this. Give me the Spanish word for what we're drinking."

Jon was amused. "Trick question. Brandy? Cognac? What?"

"*Coñac,* without the 'g.' And in what sort of container?"

"Bottle. Let's see—*bote.*"

"Almost," Max granted him. "But that could mean any bottle made of glass. When it has wine, it's called...?" She waited.

"I remember," Jon said. "It's *botella.*"

"Very good." She placed it on the tray and pointed to the coffee spoons. "This one's harder. Spoons."

Jon thought, then shook his head.

"*Cucharas.* Let's try articles of clothing. What's this?" She raised her dress above her knees, revealing a pair of slim attractive legs. Jon realized that except for two occasions, at the funeral and at the aviary, he'd only seen her in her uniform.

When he looked up, she was smiling at him with amusement. "I'm talking about the dress."

"Again, I pass."

"*Vestido.* But since you're interested in the anatomy, tell me what I'm touching." She stroked some strands of hair.

"*Pelo,*" Jon said at once. "I know because I had a crush on the girl who sat next to me in Spanish class. She was a brunette. *Morena.*"

"*Bueno.*" Max pointed to her eyes. "These?"

"*Ojos.*"

Her index finger touched the tip of his nose. "And this?"

"*Nariz.*"

"And this?" The finger moved down to his lips.

"I'm—not sure about lips."

"*Labios.* And how sure are you about this?" Her mouth opened slightly, as she placed it against his. "*Tus labios y mis labios.*" She kissed him. "*El beso,*" she whispered.

He put his arm around her. They lay back on the sofa, kissed a second time, and then a third. Her fingers stroked his chest, slipped down across his abdomen, his belt, and down again...

"Oh, *grande...grande...*"

Faintly, there was the sound of metal against metal. Max sat up.

On the far side of the room, behind them, the door was opening. Max stood and stared. "Bobito!"

In the doorway was a boy about seven. He looked at Jon with curiosity. "Who's he?"

"Come in and shut the door," Max said.

"Okay," the boy said. He pulled the key out of the lock and closed the door. He looked at Jon again. "Who are you?"

"Bobito—I'd like you to meet Mr. Wilder," she went on, flustered. "Jon… This is my son."

"Are you an agent like my mother?" the boy asked.

"No. I paint pictures," Jon said, gathering himself.

"Pictures of what?"

"Birds."

"I like Big Bird on *Sesame Street*," Bobito said. "He's not a real bird, though. I can tell."

He noticed the plate of pastries on the table. "*Pastelito!* Can I have one?"

"Just one," Max said. "Why aren't you at your grandmother's?"

"Yaya told me she was tired." He took a pastry and stuffed in his mouth.

"Was she sick?"

The boy shrugged. "She just said she was tired. We ate dinner and she fell asleep on the couch. She wanted me to go to bed. But it was early. So I took my key and came back here."

"My mother lives in the next building," Max explained to Jon.

"Is it okay if I watch *Ranchero Rangers?*" the boy asked her.

"Bobito—here's a book about Mexican birds that Mr. Wilder did." Max held up the nature guide. "He signed it for you specially. Maybe you'd like to look at it in your room."

Bobito glanced at it with disinterest. "Can I watch *Ranchero Rangers* first?"

Max sighed. "All right. But what do you say to Mr. Wilder for the book?"

The boy made a face. "Thank you." He whirled and raced down the hall out of sight.

"Not too loud," Max called after him.

"Okay!" the boy shouted back. A door closed. Moments later, the sound of hoofbeats and gunplay could be heard.

Max sat on the sofa again, this time at a discreet distance from Jon. "I'm sorry," she began. "I should have told you. Usually Bobito spends this night of the week with his grandmother. I had no way of knowing—" She left the sentence incomplete.

"He seems like a wonderful boy," Jon said.

"He is. His real name is Roberto like his father. He even looks like him. The same dark eyes."

She took a breath. "Would you like more coffee? I can fix it."

"No. This was fine."

Suddenly, Bobito reappeared. "*Mama,* are we still going to see the gunfighters tomorrow?"

"Yes." She turned to Jon. "Tomorrow, they'll reenact the shootout of the O.K. Corral in Tombstone.

It's for another movie about Wyatt Earp. A friend of mine plays one of the extras. He invited us to watch. I was supposed to work tomorrow. So I had to ask to switch my day off. Van Dine wasn't happy, but agreed.''

"You can come with us," Bobito said to Jon.

"Would you like to?" Max said. "Tombstone is only a few hours' drive. You can see the Earp brothers do a number on the Clanton gang again."

"It sounds like fun. If you don't mind," Jon said. "I can drive."

"If you don't mind doing it," Max said. "Or being here about ten-thirty."

"Not at all."

"See ya," said Bobito, and ran back to his room.

Jon rose from the sofa. "I probably should be going. Thank you for a wonderful dinner. Or what should I say—*un cena estupenda.*"

She smiled. "*Gracias, señor. Eres un buen hombre…* And I apologize."

"For what?"

"For being—confused about a lot of things. I'll see you in the morning."

"*Un momento.*" Jon said. He took her face in his hands and kissed her lingeringly on the lips. "*Un ultimo beso.*"

"*Un beso fabuloso,*" Max said softly. "*Fabuloso, Juan,*" and pressed her lips to his again.

TEN

THE MORNING WAS brilliantly clear, the sky washed to a pale blue by overnight rain showers. From Tucson, they headed east toward Benson. As they drove, Max and Bobito sang songs and played number games with license plates, and Jon told stories about places he had visited in search of birds. Leaving the interstate at Benson, they turned onto state highway 80. They passed the small town of St. David and continued south toward Tombstone. Traffic had been light for the entire trip. Then, rounding a curve several miles from Tombstone, Jon noticed a line of cars ahead that had begun to slow. Beyond them he saw flashing lights.

As they drew nearer, they discovered it was a Border Patrol roadblock. Officers stood on both sides of the highway, commanding vehicles to halt, glancing briefly into each, then waving them on.

"What, or who, are your friends after?" Jon asked Max, as he slowed his car.

Max seemed perplexed. "I haven't a clue. Van Dine didn't say anything about a roadblock today."

"Maybe because he knew it was your day off?"

"Maybe." She leaned forward and pointed.

"There's Van Dine. And that's his car. Pull off the road behind it."

Jon braked again, eased off the pavement, and stopped behind a Border Patrol car, whose roof lights were also flashing red. Max sprang out the moment Jon's car came to a stop.

"Wait here," she said, leaving the door open.

She ran ahead to where Van Dine was standing, supervising the activity. He saw her and gave her a broad smile. Several times Max gestured toward the line of cars. Each time Van Dine sought to pacify her, even putting a hand on her shoulder with apparent fatherly affection.

Beyond them, on both sides of the highway, a half-dozen other Border Patrol officers went about their business, raising their hands for vehicles to halt, checking the occupants inside, and occasionally asking to see licenses. Among them was Agent Martinez. Unlike his colleagues, who had mastered the technique, Martinez took time more time than necessary with each step, causing traffic to back up along the road.

Max returned to Jon's car and climbed in. "You were right. Van Dine claims he didn't mention anything about the roadblock since he knew I'd be away."

"Did he tell you what they're looking for?"

Max nodded. "That puzzles me, too."

"What do you mean?"

"He said there was a tip The Hawk was in the area," Max told him. "If he's right, I wouldn't have taken the day off. He knows how much I want to be there when they catch him." She stared at Van Dine glumly. "Too late now. Let's go."

Jon put the car in gear and swung onto the highway. From the shoulder where he stood, Van Dine gave a friendly wave.

IN SPITE OF the delay, they arrived in Tombstone precisely at high noon, a fact that Jon thought was ironically appropriate. After a pleasant lunch at The Shootout Café, they walked through the town, visiting the old courthouse and gallows on Toughnut Street as well as Boot Hill Cemetery, all reminders of Tombstone's sometime violent past. Moving on to Allen Street, they passed the O.K. Corral, discovered the office of *The Tombstone Epitaph*, the town's first newspaper, and ended their sightseeing at the Silver Nugget Ice Cream Parlor, where Jon bought ice cream cones for all of them.

Now they sat outside the ice cream parlor, while they ate the cones. Bobito was the first to finish his.

"I wish I could've been there when they shot the Clanton gang," he said, leaping to his feet.

He whirled. "Pow! Pow! Pow!" Bobito fired with his index fingers at a lamppost. "Take that, Johnny Ringo! Curly Bill—you're dead!"

"You're a faster draw than Marshal Earp was," Jon said.

"Tombstone's marshal wasn't Wyatt Earp," the boy corrected him. "His brother Virgil was." He whirled again, crouched, and fired finger salvos at a hitching post along the street. "Gotcha, Billy Clanton!"

"Holster your guns, pardner, and sit," Max told her son.

Directly opposite them was The Bird Cage Theater, a relic from the 1880s that continued to survive.

Bobito pointed to the sign. "Why is it called the Bird Cage Theater?" he asked his mother.

"Because when it first opened it was where men went to dance and gamble," she told him. "And there were women in big bird cages hanging from the ceiling, who called down to them."

"Why did they do that?" the boy wondered. "Were they being friendly?"

Max glanced at Jon. "Yes. They were being friendly."

"Tombstone must have been quite a place in its day," Jon ventured.

"After silver was discovered here, it was the most important city between San Francisco and El Paso," Max said. "Its real industry these days is tourists. The Earps and Doc Holliday probably wouldn't recognize the place."

Bobito turned to Jon. "Do you know who Doc Holliday's girlfriend was?"

"Can't say that I do," Jon admitted. "Tell me."

"Big Nose Kate," the boy said. "She was a soiled dove."

"A what?" Max said, surprised.

"A *whore*," Bobito told her, with no understanding of the word. "They were called soiled doves."

Max gave Jon another amused glance. "I bet that's one bird you don't have in your nature guides."

They were interrupted by of a tall man in his late thirties dressed in black suit and flowered waistcoat, who waved from across the street. As he came toward them, Jon saw he was carrying a black hat. On the leather belt around his waist, a holstered gun was visible.

Max returned the wave. "Hi, Tom."

Bobito saw him, too, and began firing with his fingers. "Pow! Pow!"

"You just shot the mayor of Tombstone," the man told Bobito. "The Earps aren't going to like that much." He looked at Max and smiled. "I'm very glad you came."

"Tom, I'd like you to meet Jon Wilder," she said. "Jon, this is Tom Douglas."

"The same name as the bird guy?" Tom asked, shaking hands.

"I am the bird guy," Jon said. "Are you a birder?"

"When I have time," Tom said.

"This spring Tom took me to Mount Lemmon to see birds," Bobito said.

"Tom is a fellow agent in the Yuma station," Max explained. "We've worked together on a few assignments."

"Today is also my day off," he said to Jon. "So I'm an extra in the film. That's why I'm duded up like this." He pointed to the waistcoat and the hat.

"Is your gun real?" Bobito asked him, pointing to the .45 Dakota at his hip.

"No. None of the actors carry real guns."

"Where is the movie being filmed?" Jon wondered.

"Several blocks away," Tom said, "there's a film set of Tombstone in the 1880s. The locals use it to stage reenactments of the O.K. Corral shootout for tourists. But it's used for movies, too. The one they're shooting now is Japanese; sort of a sushi western. They're about to film the confrontation of the Earps and Clanton gang."

Tom checked his watch. "It's almost two. I better get back."

"You also better take off your wristwatch, Mayor," Max advised. "It's not exactly period."

"Good idea," Tom agreed. He unclasped the watch and handed it to her. "Would you mind holding it? If I put it in the pocket of my costume, I'll forget it."

"Sure." She took the watch and slipped it in her purse. "You go ahead. We'll be there soon."

"Thanks," Tom said. "I'll see you." He turned and started off.

Max, Jon, and Bobito also joined the crowd that was making their way toward Fourth Street, where the filming was taking place. They had reached Allen Street and Fifth, when a man strode around the corner, directly in their path. He stopped and stared at them.

"Howdy, Mr. Wilder," he said after a breath. It was Billy Ketchum. He was wearing Levi's, boots, and a Stetson hat. He glanced at Max and Bobito, then turned back to Jon. "Sorry to be in a rush. Nice to see you."

He looked fleetingly again at Max and touched his Stetson. "Ma'am."

The next moment he was past them, his boots thundering along the boardwalk planks. Max watched him go.

"Billy Ketchum certainly knows how to do the Texas two-step when he wants to," she commented. "I'm surprised he didn't break into a run."

"You know Ketchum?" Jon asked.

"And he knows me," Max said. "I arrested him. Actually, it was the police and I. But I did most of the investigation that led to it."

They resumed walking.

"What was he arrested for?" Jon asked her.

"Involuntary servitude is the official term."

"You mean slavery?"

"It sounds bizarre, I know," Max said. "But in the Southwest, it often involves illegals from Mexico and Central America. And theirs isn't the slavery of the Old South a hundred fifty years ago. This is almost worse."

"What happened?"

"For years, Ketchum had been bringing girls into the U.S. illegally, usually by placing ads in Mexican newspapers. They were supposed to work as housekeepers and cooks. The ads promised them good wages, opportunities for education, even citizenship. But once they were here, they became virtual prisoners in Ketchum's house. And household duties were the least of what they had to do. Seems Ketchum has a very hearty appetite for *señoritas*."

"Didn't any of the women go to the authorities?"

"Most wanted to, I'm sure," Max said. "But Ketchum kept them so intimidated and afraid, none did. Finally, he beat one girl to the point she had to be taken to the hospital. Her bruises were so bad when she arrived, the staff nicknamed her Ponchita Purple. That's when we and the police were notified."

"Was Ketchum indicted?"

"With the speed of light."

"And?"

"Whether out of fear or shame, the girl refused to press charges against him. Her explanation was that she'd fallen down the stairs. Since Ketchum lived in a one-floor house, it made no sense. But there was nothing we could do. Ketchum hired a good lawyer and got off with a fine. Injustice triumphed."

"Is he out of the slave trade now?" Jon asked her.

"We're not sure," Max told him. "We're not sure."

A large crowd of onlookers had already gathered at the location where the film was being shot, kept out of camera range by security guards. Around the area were massive lights, reflectors, and four cameras to record the action, one of them mounted on a crane. A jumble of cables encircled the perimeter. In the center of the street a small Asian man wearing sunglasses and a baseball cap was waving his arms and shouting loud commands at no one in particular. Jon was sure he was the director. At a distance from him, the actors who portrayed the Earps and Clanton gang were chatting amiably.

Max touched Jon's arm. "Tom said there's a place away from the crowd where we can stand."

She led them to several long catering tables on which coffee urns, trays of pastries, and fresh fruit had been laid out. Gathered around them, members of the film crew drained their cups, tossed them into bins, and ambled back to work.

As they dispersed, Max pointed to spot behind the coffee urns. "We should be able to see everything from there."

The activity resumed. As the crew returned to their equipment, the giant lights blazed suddenly and technicians took their places behind cameras and sound recorders. The Earps and Clanton gang shook hands and walked in opposite directions, taking their positions on the street. Finally, the director ceased his shouting and hurried to the camera that had been mounted on the crane. He sat beside the cameraman and held a viewfinder to his eye.

There were calls for quiet on the set. Someone shouted "Speed." The scene was noted on the clapperboard, the sticks were slapped together, and the crane with its two occupants began to rise.

Facing one another at a distance of a dozen yards, the Earps, Doc Holliday, and the three outlaws of the Clanton gang began their final confrontation. That it wasn't taking place inside a corral but in the middle of the street didn't seem to bother anyone.

Abruptly, guns were drawn by the combatants; there was a fusillade of fire from both sides. Bobito pressed his hands against his ears and stared as blood appeared on Doc Holliday's left shirtsleeve and on the chests of Billy and Ike Clanton. The extras, Tom among them, had already ducked for cover into buildings or behind barrels and hitching posts.

Total silence followed.

The camera crane descended to the street and the director bounded off. There was more waving and commands. The actors sidled back to their original positions. Doc Holliday and Ike and Billy Clanton were provided with clean shirts. The scene would be reshot.

Waiting for the action to begin again, Jon looked at Max and her young son. Her arm lay gently around his shoulders. Bobito's head leaned against her hip. The strong and loving bond between the two was obvious. As if aware that Jon was watching them, the boy turned his head and smiled up at him.

"Fantastic, huh?" Bobito said.

Jon returned the smile. "Fantastic," he agreed.

From doors and behind objects, extras also reappeared, smoothing and adjusting their costumes for the second take. On the boardwalk just outside the Rusty Spike Saloon, Tom Douglas inspected his six-shooter and holstered it.

Suddenly Jon saw another figure he hadn't noticed earlier. Kneeling on the roof of the two-story building housing the saloon, was a person dressed in the costume of a cowboy: yoke shirt, leather vest, and kerchief. A broad-brimmed cowboy hat had been pulled forward and down, so that the upper portion of the face could not be seen. The person held a rifle.

More shouts, lights and action, and the scene began again.

This time Bobito decided he could brave the gunfire. Still, to fortify himself, he reached toward the tray of pastries in front of him.

The Earps and Clantons now drew their guns and fired. Gun smoke enveloped them and bodies fell. Just then, Jon glanced down and saw coffee spewing from both sides of an urn. Suddenly, the rail of the hitching post beside him splintered, as a bullet ripped apart the wood.

"Get down!" he shouted to Max.

A third shot struck the doughnut Bobito had been reaching for. Jon grabbed him, as Max turned. He pulled her to the ground. It was too late.

"I'm hit," she said, almost matter-of-factly.

Jon's hand went around her shoulder and he felt a stickiness.

Dazed and confused, Bobito started to sob.

Jon looked at his own hand and saw that it was red with Max's blood. Max reached to her left shoulder, feeling the blood also as the dark stain spread across her blouse.

"I'm hit," she said again. "It hurts."

Chaos was surrounding them. People shouted. Footsteps were running everywhere.

"Don't try to move," Jon said. He reached up, found a wad of paper napkins on the table, and pressed them to the wound.

"What happened?" somebody was asking.

Jon looked up. A young security officer stood over

them. "What happened to her?" He was ghostly white.

"Someone shot at us," Jon told him.

"Couldn't have," the young officer said. "Nobody was using real guns."

"*Somebody* was, damn it!" Jon stood and faced him. "Get an ambulance!"

The officer looked at Max again, as if he would be sick.

"*Do it!*" Jon said.

The young man seized his radio and began speaking.

More guards had already surrounded them, some shouting orders to the growing crowd. Jon saw Tom Douglas pushing his way them, against orders to stop. Behind him was an older man, dressed as a shopkeeper.

"I'm a doctor," the man said. He knelt beside Max and, with a knife he'd taken from the table, began cutting away fabric from the wound.

Seeing Tom, Bobito clung to him, continuing to sob. Tom held the boy close and comforted him.

"What happened?" Tom asked Jon at last.

"Somebody was shooting at us."

"Who?"

"I don't know. But just before the actors did the scene again, I saw someone with a rifle on the roof above the Rusty Spike Saloon."

"I was below it, just outside the doors!" Tom said, incredulous.

"Did anybody with a rifle enter or leave?" Jon asked.

"Yes. A few. But they were extras in the movie, also. And their guns were props."

"Not this one," Jon said.

"You're sure he was above the Rusty Spike Saloon?" Tom wanted to know.

"Yes."

Both men turned and looked up at the building's roof.

The roof was empty.

ELEVEN

THE DOOR OF the hospital room was closed when Jon arrived. Even so, he could hear voices—Max's, soft and somewhat weak; Van Dine's, crisp and resolute. He sat on a bench opposite the room and waited.

A nurse appeared along the hall. She went inside and closed the door. Moments later it reopened and Van Dine stepped out. He saw Jon and looked at him with an expression of relief.

"At least you're all right," Van Dine said. "Somebody told me you'd been hit along with Max."

"It wasn't for lack of trying on the shooter's part," Jon said.

"We're going to get 'em, Jon. I promise that. Have you given a statement to the police?"

"To the Cochise County sheriff's officers, yes," Jon said.

"I may also ask Agent Martinez to talk with you, if you don't mind."

"Not at all."

Van Dine inclined his head in the direction of the room. "You can probably go in when the nurse leaves."

He walked a few steps, then turned back and faced

Jon again. "A word of caution. After what occurred today, I'd watch my back." He started for the elevator at the far end of the hall.

The door of Max's room remained shut. So Jon sat on the bench and waited some more. The wall clock showed it was several minutes after five.

It was still hard to believe so much had happened in the last hours. Soon after being wounded, Max had been transported by ambulance to the hospital in Benson. From there, she'd been airlifted by helicopter to the Tucson Medical Center on the east side of the city. Tom had accompanied her on both trips. Jon, on the other hand, had looked after Bobito; first, assuring him his mother would be all right, then driving the boy back to Tucson and to his grandmother's apartment.

The door of Max's room opened and the nurse appeared. She was about to close the door when she saw Jon and nodded. He thanked the nurse and strode across the hall.

As he entered the room, Max was lying with her head slightly elevated. Her left shoulder was heavily bandaged and an intravenous line was connected to her lower arm.

She smiled. "Hi."

"How are you feeling?"

"Lousy and lucky both," Max said. "At least I didn't end up like the Clanton gang."

"I just saw Van Dine in the hall," Jon told her. "He got here quickly."

Max nodded. "He said he was already headed back

to Tucson when he received the call that I'd been wounded."

"He seems determined to get the ones who did this."

"He doesn't like people taking potshots at his agents," Max said.

"Did he have any information on who might have done the shooting?"

Max tried to shake her head and winced. "No. But he wants to find Tom and ask him a few questions."

"Does he think Tom had something to do with it?"

"I doubt it. He's just covering his bases. Tom was the person who invited us to Tombstone, but I know he couldn't be involved."

"Where is Tom now?"

"In the cafeteria, I hope, getting something to eat. He said he'd be back." She managed a small laugh. "I'm sure he will. I still have his watch."

"Is there anything I can get you while I'm here?" Jon asked.

"Maybe a new shoulder. I told Van Dine to take me out of the intersector softball game on Saturday. Otherwise, the doctors tell me I'll be fine. The bullet hit soft tissue but no bones. That's the good news." She frowned. "The bad news is he took me off the case."

"Completely?"

"Yes. He also told me I should take a long vacation. He said that given Roberto's death and now this, I've had a very rocky year. Besides, he feels that the smugglers have probably upped the bounty on me, and he doesn't want me put in jeopardy again. Next time, he said, the shooter might not miss.''

"It could have been me they were shooting at," Jon said.

"I thought of that," Max said. She frowned again. "By the way, my mother called. Thanks for looking after Bobito. How was he?"

"Upset at first. But driving back, we shared more stories about birds. By the time we got to Tucson, he was a lot better."

Max reached for his hand and squeezed it. "I told you, you're a good guy, Jon."

The door of the room opened. Tom stood in the doorway. He looked awful: fatigue showed on his face and he was pale. What Jon also saw was that he was still dressed in the costume he had worn in Tombstone. Even the prop gun remained holstered at his belt. If he'd been to the hospital cafeteria, Jon thought, he must have received immediate attention.

Tom looked at Max, then Jon. "I can come back," he said.

"That's all right," Jon said. "I ought to go."

"No, stay. I'll wait outside," Tom said, and closed the door.

Jon turned back to the bed. "I really should be going, anyway. And maybe Van Dine's right. I know you don't want to give up the case, but it could be dangerous if you continue."

"That sounds like my advice to you the first time we met," Max said. "But even if I do, I have a feeling you'll keep at it. I don't want you going solo on me, Jon.''

Jon said nothing. Max read his expression.

''I mean it. I don't want something happening to you on my account.''

''I won't let it,'' he told her.

''That's not what I said. No heroics. Promise me.''

He bent down and kissed her on the cheek. ''Get some rest. I'll call you in the morning.''

She smiled. ''I hope so.''

Jon left the room. Tom, who had been seated on the bench opposite, rose and went inside.

Jon walked to the elevator. He pushed the down arrow and waited. At last, the elevator reached the floor and the doors separated. Jon stepped in. There was one other passenger. It was Luis Cardenal. If he was as surprised as Jon, he didn't show it; the man's saturnine eyes appeared expressionless.

''How do you do, Mr. Wilder?'' Cardenal said. ''We only seem to meet at times of sadness, do we not?''

''What do you mean?''

''At the Floreses' home after the funeral and at Voss's house the night he died. Today is sad as well. A close friend suffered a massive heart attack last night while at his home. I believe you know him. Antonio Salera. I'm sure it was brought on by the stress of the events.''

Jon was startled. ''What events?''

''I gather you don't know then,'' Cardenal said. ''He was indicted yesterday.''

"For what?"

"Drug smuggling. It seems the authorities found traces of cocaine hidden in sections of that antique car of his."

"The one he rode in during the parade in Santa Rita?"

"He travels with it on personal appearances," Cardenal said. "The police claim he used it for the transportation of narcotics. I hope they're wrong. I view smuggling as a contemptible endeavor, whether its drugs or human beings. Wouldn't you agree?"

"Of course."

The elevator slowed and stopped at the ground floor. The doors parted.

Luis Cardenal gave a polite nod. "Have a good day, Mr. Wilder."

He stepped from the elevator and was gone.

THE RAIN CAME as a surprise.

It began just as Jon left the hospital. When he'd arrived an hour earlier, the sky had been an azure blue. Now dark clouds were sweeping in from the southwest. Before he'd crossed the parking lot, large, sullen drops were falling everywhere.

He drove out of the parking lot and headed west on Grant Road in the direction of the interstate. Within several blocks, the rain was so intense the traffic lights were difficult to see. Jon turned the windshield wipers to their fastest setting. Even then, the sweeping blades did little to increase his visibility.

By the time, he reached the entrance ramp to I-10,

his only bearings were the rear lights of the truck ahead. He also checked the rearview mirror to see who was behind him. He could faintly make out the front end of a white Chevy Blazer. Only one headlight was working. He recalled seeing a white Blazer with a smashed headlight in the hospital parking lot when he'd arrived. He'd also noticed it had been covered with a fine layer of dust, as if it had been driven through a sandstorm recently. If it was the same vehicle, this rain would wash it clean.

South of the city, where Interstate 10 swung east, Jon turned onto I-19. To his right, he could just see the blurry outline of Mission San Xavier del Bac, its gleaming white stucco walls obscured by mist. A short distance ahead was the six-lane bridge crossing over the Santa Cruz River. Broad and dry most of the year, Emilio had told him of a catastrophic flood in 1983. The force and volume of the water that had rushed through the riverbed had collapsed the bridge, taking with it pilings, girders, and tons of concrete, and leaving many of the massive steel guardrails grotesquely twisted in its wake. Once over the bridge, Jon took a breath and slowed his car.

Most of the other drivers displayed caution, too, keeping a safe distance from each other. Now and then, a large tractor trailer truck swept by them on the inside lane, throwing up cascades of water as it went. Where the interstate crossed under another road, some cars had pulled onto the shoulder, sheltered by the bridge above them, to wait out the storm.

Jon passed the sign that announced Duval Mines

Road. The pickup truck was still ahead of him, the Chevy Blazer just behind.

Soon he saw the sign for Cottonwood Springs, then the towns of Continental and Arivaca Junction. Then came Wyatt's Spur and Santa Rita. Rio Lobo was still seven miles to the south.

Lightning coursed through the sky and thunder could be heard. As if contributing to the dramatic sound and light show, fresh torrents of rain poured down. Surprisingly, it was that moment that the driver of the Chevy Blazer chose to show his nerve. Swinging out, he raced past Jon and the cars in front of him, the Blazer's rear lights disappearing almost instantly from sight.

Finally, the sign for Rio Lobo loomed ahead. The road leading to the Wolfshead Inn was opposite the exit ramp. Jon slowed the car and eased off, stopping at the bottom of the ramp. Following the signs, he started up the entrance road. A half-mile farther there would be the small, two-lane bridge that spanned the Rio Lobo—the River of the Wolf—itself. Like the Santa Cruz and Rillito rivers, the Rio Lobo had been dry each time Jon had driven over it. But he recalled reading a warning to guests in the general information that during the monsoon season, from early July to mid-September, rain could fall at a rate of three to four inches an hour, and urging caution from flash floods in low-lying areas. Jon guessed the Rio Lobo had a bit of water in it now.

The traffic cones that blocked the road ahead confirmed it.

There were five of them, each one a dirty, DayGlo orange, placed across the road. A large road sign, also orange with a black arrow, leaned against the center cone. The arrow pointed to another road that went off to the right.

The road was narrower and covered with coarse gravel; Jon guessed it was probably a service road that led up to the inn. Presumably, it avoided the Rio Lobo, and the inn's management had decided to divert all traffic onto it for safety's sake.

The road was bumpy but negotiable as Jon continued on. Soon, however, the gravel became looser and more porous, the road crowning in the center, which left muddy swales on both sides. The thought began to cross Jon's mind that he should turn around and head back to the main road. He also knew that even if he'd tried such a maneuver, it would be impossible. Turning the car would have put the front wheels into a ditch either way. How deep the ditches were he didn't know.

Jon stopped the car. Peering through the windshield, he saw lights in the distance. The inn was only several hundred yards away. He put the car in gear and drove ahead.

Almost at once, the terrain became increasingly uneven: dropping, rising, and dropping again, giving him the sense he was driving on a giant washboard. The car crested another hill and started down—when Jon saw what awaited him.

No more than twenty feet below him was a swirling turbulence of water, sand, and silt that had seized everything before it: cactus, mesquite, ocotillo, even rocks.

Jon slammed on the brakes. Nothing. Tractionless, the car continued sliding down the hill.

He wrenched the steering wheel hard to the left as far as it would go. The car lurched sideways, slipping off the road and stopping momentarily. Then slowly it resumed its downward slide.

Jon whipped off his seat belt and flung open the door. Immediately it swung back against his wrist with total force.

He kicked open the door, this time holding it with his foot. Grabbing the frame of the door above, he threw himself out of the car. Moments later he was facedown in the mud.

He turned his head to the side, searching for the car. A few yards down the hill, he saw it. The driver's door still open, it suddenly rolled onto its roof, slipped into the violent torrent, and was gone.

TWELVE

"NO. ABSOLUTELY NO," Emilio repeated. "The idea is crazy."

"Hear me out," Jon said.

"I heard. I listened. Now, excuse me while I open the shop."

Emilio twisted the key in the padlock of the wrought-iron gates at the entrance of Flores Importers and swung them back.

"I have a plan," Jon went on, when the gates were set in place.

"I'm sure you do," Emilio shot back, "and this time it will get you killed. It could be very dangerous for you to travel into Mexico."

"It's getting very dangerous for me right here," Jon said.

Emilio grunted, opened the doors of the shop itself, and went inside. Jon followed him.

Emilio halted, glowering. "And what are you doing here at seven in the morning? After your adventures yesterday, it's *you* who should be in the hospital. How did you get here, by the way? I thought your car was swept off in a flood."

"It was. The car rental people furnished me another."

"Well, keep this one on dry land. And don't try driving into Mexico. For that you need Mexican insurance."

"I didn't intend to drive myself," Jon told him.

"Oh? Do you have a chauffeur?"

"I was hoping you."

"*Me?* Now I know you're crazy." Emilio threw up his hands and started for his office at the rear.

Again, Jon followed close behind. "Look, you're in the export-import business. You travel in and out of Mexico a couple times a week transporting things."

"Things, yes. I don't transport people."

Emilio unlocked his office door. Once in, he made a circuit of the room, opening the blinds and turning on the lights.

"And sometimes you have others riding with you in the truck to help with the heavy pieces."

"Yes. But they are young men from the stockroom," Emilio informed him. "All are Hispanic, under twenty-five, and lift weights in their spare time. Besides, most guards on both sides of the border know their names. They're recognized on sight."

Emilio unlocked the file cabinets and finally his desk. He sat and turned on his computer. "But just suppose that you succeed. What will you do then?"

"I'll let you know when I get back."

"*If* you get back. Have you told Agent Montoya what you have in mind?"

"I'll call her at the hospital before I go."

"And say what?"

"That I expect to be away for a few days."

Emilio swung around in his desk chair. "I tell you this, my friend. After Angélica and the others died, I would have done anything I could to know more about the smugglers. Who murdered them and, in particular, to know who is their leader, who allows such deaths to happen. But I'm convinced that even if I know their names, I can't bring them to justice. No one can."

"Are you driving into Mexico today?" Jon asked him.

"Yes. But without you as my passenger." Emilio swung back to the computer and began typing.

"What time are you leaving?"

"At nine. Alone."

"What's your destination?"

"Hermosillo."

"And from what I saw waiting on the loading dock, you'll be transporting furniture. Chairs. Cabinets. A chest of drawers."

The other frowned. "Don't even think it, Jon."

"The cabinets I saw are tall. Can you remove the shelves?"

Emilio stopped typing and looked up. "Yes, I can. And no, I won't. If your idea is to hide inside, you might as well be in a coffin when they catch you. In fact, it will save them the expense of finding one before they bury you."

"But you know the border guards. They like you,"

Jon went on. "You've told me all they do is read your cargo manifest, match it with the items in the truck, and wave you through."

"Most of the time, yes," Emilio agreed. "But sometimes an officer appears who I don't know and who does not know me. Usually he's young or just been transferred to the post. Last month there was a customs guard, a young Mexican, probably of rural background, who insisted I show him my entire load of terra cotta pots. He said he wanted to be sure the pots didn't contain drugs. What he really wanted was a bribe. When I refused, he took the pots and dropped them one by one onto the pavement, breaking all of them. His fellow guards just laughed."

"I have another idea," Jon said.

"I don't want to know it."

"Does Father Flannery say early mass?"

"In the summer, yes. It's starting now," Emilio said, looking at the clock. "More people would rather attend mass at this hour than in the middle of the day, when it's too hot."

"What time is it over?"

"Maybe seven-thirty," Emilio suggested. "It's not long."

"Then I could see him afterward."

"I presume. He should be there all day," Emilio said. "He could give you absolution."

"Absolution for what?"

Emilio lifted his eyes. "For whatever sins of foolhardiness you are about to commit."

WRAPPED IN packing quilts, the teakwood cabinet was hoisted by Emilio and the young man onto the bed of the pickup truck.

"Gracias," Emilio said to him. He gestured to a pair of wooden chairs still on the loading dock. *"Las sillas, por favor."*

The young man jumped from the truck and picked up a chair. Emilio took it and secured it in a space beside the cabinet. The young man turned back for the second chair. But instead of taking it, he crossed himself and stared at the two priests coming toward them through the alleyway.

Emilio looked also. As they approached, he saw that one was Father Flannery, his white cane beating a tattoo against the stones. The second priest, dressed in black, as well, was carrying a small leather case in his left hand. Seeing Emilio, he raised his hand in a blessing.

"I'll be damned," Emilio said. "Is that you, Jon?"

"Verily," Jon answered. "And I will spare you damnation."

"Good morning, Emilio," Father Flannery said cheerily. "I'd like you to meet Father Nicholas Finch, S.J. The S.J. stands for Suddenly Jesuit. He's about to return to missionary work in Mexico."

"You look like twins," Emilio told them. "Black jacket and trousers. Roman collar. Black shoes. Except Father Finch's sleeves are about three inches too short. And the outfit has seen better days."

"It comes from working in the fields with the peasants," Jon said. "I think the threadbare look bespeaks my vow of poverty."

"The clothes are an old set I was holding onto," Father Flannery explained. "When Jon came to me and told me what he had in mind, I thought of them. Fortunately, Jon and I are pretty much the same size, except for the arms. But once we're into Mexico, he can take off the jacket."

"And what exactly is your mission, Father?" Emilio asked Jon.

"To ask questions. To learn names."

"How long do you expect this work to take?"

"I have no way of knowing," Jon admitted. "With God's help, I hope to be back in the United States within a week."

"Everyone, except for God, needs a visa or a tourist card to stay in Mexico," Emilio informed him.

"Again, thanks to Father Flannery, I have one."

Jon reached into an inner pocket of the jacket and produced a leather case. He opened it and showed it to Emilio. The face on the official-looking visa was Jon's, wearing the clerical collar and black shirt.

Emilio shook his head. "And how did you obtain it, may I ask?"

Father Flannery smiled. "You might consider it the devil's work. But a parishoner who lives near the church was convicted years ago of falsifying documents. He's since reformed. But when I told him what was needed he agreed. Using my visa and Jon's picture, he came up with this."

Emilio seemed skeptical. "The border guards may be suspicious that I'm traveling with priests."

"By serving as our transportation into Mexico,

you're serving God," Father Flannery replied. "On one hand, you're helping Father Finch resume his ministry. As for myself, it's allowed me to accept the invitation of a seminary colleague to visit him in Magdelena. Also, it'll give Jon and me a chance to talk. In our hurry to be here before you left, we didn't have the opportunity."

Emilio studied Jon carefully and finally pointed down to the black shoes. "One matter you must attend to is to make certain that your shoes are wiped and polished, *Padre*. In the desert, we all live with dust. But people expect priest's shoes to be clean."

"I'll keep it in mind."

"And do you know what saint's day it is today?" Emilio said. "Someone may ask you."

"Saint Jerome," Jon said.

Emilio glanced at Father Flannery. The priest concurred.

Emilio looked back at Jon. "It may be the feast day of Saint Jerome. But the saint who you should pray to is Saint Jude."

"Why?" Jon asked.

"Because he is the saint of the impossible." Emilio opened the door of the pickup. "All right, you two blackbirds—get into the truck."

THEY DROVE in silence. Morning sunlight quickly filled the valley. Approaching the northern section of Nogales, Arizona, small houses began to appear on the hillsides. At a distance, Jon could see the trucking terminals where massive eighteen-wheelers sat in rows, their trailers bearing the names of shippers from Tegucigalpa to Vancouver.

Emilio was the first to speak. *"Bienvenido a Mexico,"* he said. He pointed to the arch announcing above the border crossing into Mexico.

They cleared U.S. and Mexico customs without incident and continued south toward the town of Magdelena. Beyond Nogales, Mexico, the small, well-kept adobe houses gave way to mobile homes on cinder blocks and, finally, to dwellings of sheet metal and tar paper around which children, goats, and chickens roamed at will. Once on the broad, four-lane highway, the names of towns flew by—Agua Zarca, Cibuta, Imuris, San Ignacio.

As the high desert stretched away toward distant hills, Jon was tempted to put his head back and close his eyes. Then he saw Emilio glance furtively into the side mirror. His hands tightened on the wheel and the pickup truck began to slow.

"Is there a problem?" Father Flannery asked, curious.

Emilio said nothing. He brought the truck to a stop along the right shoulder of the road. A moment later, a white car pulled ahead of them and stopped as well. The two inside appeared to be in uniform. But there were no official markings on the car.

"Our luck may have run out," Emilio said in a low voice. He opened the glove compartment and reached into it for documents.

"Is it the police?" Jon asked him.

"I don't know," Emilio admitted. "It could be the

judiciales. Or maybe customs or narcotics. We'll know soon enough."

A squat, balding officer stepped from the driver's side of the car and walked slowly toward the truck.

Emilio lowered his window. *"Buenos dias,"* he said.

"Buenos dias," the officer responded. *"Inmigración."* He said a few more words in Spanish and gestured to the rear of the truck.

"He wants to see what I'm carrying," Emilio explained. "Excuse me." He picked up the cargo manifest, climbed out of the cab, and went with the officer to the back of the truck.

But Jon's attention was again focused on the car ahead. From the other side, a second officer appeared. He was extremely tall and in his twenties, with a large mustache. He started toward them, a macho swagger to his walk.

"Here comes another officer," Jon muttered to Father Flannery. "He looks like trouble."

Jon lowered the window on his side.

"Identificación," the tall officer said brusquely through the window.

Father Flannery pulled his wallet from an inside pocket and handed it across. The officer snapped it open, gave it a cursory look, and handed it back.

"Tarjeta de turista," he demanded of the priest. "Tourist card," he repeated in English.

"I'll only be in Magdelena for the day," Father Flannery said pleasantly but firmly. "I don't need a tourist card."

The officer frowned. He looked at Jon. "And you? Will you also be in Magdelena for the day?"

"No. I'm going farther," Jon told him. He withdrew the visa Father Flannery had given him and presented it to the officer.

The officer flipped through it. "You've spent some time in Mexico," he said, not looking up.

"I have."

The other studied the small photo in the visa, then peered at Jon. "I've seen you somewhere," he said, finally.

"I've visited several parishes around southern Arizona," Jon said. "Also, as the visa shows, I was in Mexico last year." It was part of a story Jon had constructed, in the event he was required to explain the information on the visa.

"I don't attend the parishes in southern Arizona," the man said. "It was somewhere else." He pointed to the black leather case on Jon's lap. "What are you carrying in that?"

Jon felt his mouth go dry. He lifted the case and held it out the window to the officer. When Father Flannery had given him the forged visa that morning, he'd also given Jon the case, which he said priests often carry. At the time, Jon hadn't looked inside it, thinking of it only as a prop.

The officer had unclasped the case and thrust a hand inside. He felt around and took out an object: a small chalice made of silver. It was followed by a matching silver paten, a white surplice, and a missal. The officer stuffed them back in the case and returned the case to Jon, unclasped.

He looked at Jon one final time, then turned and walked back to the car.

Jon took a long deep breath. "He's gone. Thank God."

"This morning," Father Flannery said in a low voice, "you told me you hoped to link up with the smugglers. Is that still your intention?"

"Yes. And travel back across the border?"

"And how do you expect to find these smugglers?" the other asked.

"I thought I'd travel as far as Hermosillo with Emilio," Jon said. "In Hermosillo, I'll begin to make inquiries."

"That could take days," Father Flannery said.

"I know."

"I have a better suggestion. I've heard stories about a place from some of my congregation, who came as illegals. Several miles south of Cuesta de Cobre is a small town. It's no more than a crossroads, really—a cantina, several stores, a mechanic's shop and *gasolinera* that doubles as a bus stop. Every day in the late afternoon, a bus arrives there to refuel. But while the driver's getting gasoline, the bus also takes on passengers, most of them illegals heading north. The police know about it, but they're paid off, so the bus is never detained. Still, it could be risky. I've heard stories of mistreatment."

"How do I get included with the travelers?" Jon asked.

"First, go to the cantina and say you're there to meet a man named Javier. Most illegals use the story that Javier is a cousin; the man must have the largest extended family in Mexico. But you're a gringo and a priest, so your story will have to be different."

"I've already thought of one," Jon said.

"Good. What about money?"

"I have American money. Also, I exchanged some dollars for pesos last night at the hotel."

"Also good. And necessary for the trip. Javier will ask for a down payment of several hundred dollars. If he trusts you."

"If he doesn't?"

"One of his real cousins will take you to a nearby river and shoot you," Father Flannery said. "So make sure your story is believable."

"To say the least."

"After the bus picks up its passengers, it heads toward the Arizona border. At a town near the border, the illegals get off and are met by the first group of *coyotes,* who drive them into the United States."

"In pickup trucks, I suppose."

"No, drive them on foot, like cattle," Father Flannery said. "When they're across, they're met by a second group who transports them farther north. Finally, they're brought to safe houses around Tucson. Keep in mind that every time your escort changes, they'll want money."

"What if—" Jon started to say.

But Emilio and the squat officer suddenly appeared

beside the cab. Emilio climbed into the cab and closed the door.

"*Gracias,*" he said to the officer.

The man waved a hand and started toward the car.

The truck continued on. Entering Magdelena, they drove to the center of town and stopped beside a schoolyard adjacent to a Catholic church. In the yard, a young priest was refereeing a boys' soccer game.

"I see a priest wearing glasses," Emilio said.

"That's him," Father Flannery said. "Honk the horn."

Emilio did so. The priest in the playground turned in the direction of the truck and waved.

"Your friend knows you're here," Emilio told Father Flannery.

"Let me walk with you to the yard," Jon offered.

He and the priest climbed out of the cab.

"I'll pick you up about five on my way back from Hermosillo," Emilio called after Father Flannery.

"Fine. I'll be waiting," Father Flannery called back.

He and Jon crossed the street and started toward the school. In the yard, the priest called half time in the soccer game.

"I know I don't need to say it, Jon," Father Flannery told him. "But good luck. And try to avoid performing any sacraments, even if you're asked. It could be a giveaway you're not a priest."

"I'll keep it in mind," Jon said. "By the way, the town where I'm supposed to board the bus. Does it have a name?"

"The name listed on the map is San Miguel de la Montaña. But everyone, including the residents, calls it Las Pulgas."

"Las Pulgas? What does that mean in Spanish?" Jon asked.

"Quite literally, the fleas."

"The fleas?"

Father Flannery gave him a wry smile. "When you arrive, you'll see that it's well named."

THIRTEEN

"TURN OFF AT the next exit, would you?" Jon asked.

Emilio glanced over. "You want me to take you to Cuesta de Cobre? There's nothing there."

"Actually, I'm looking for a town called San Miguel de la Montaña."

A snort came from Emilio. "There's even more of nothing in that place."

"I want to stop, anyway."

"Suit yourself, *Padre*. San Miguel it is." Emilio returned his attention to the road.

Emilio eased off the highway when the exit ramp came into view. At the bottom of the ramp, there were two wooden arrows. One pointed right with CUESTA DE COBRE painted on it in black letters. A second arrow pointed to the left. The shaft of the arrow was mostly missing, so that all that remained of the town's name was SAN MIGU. Emilio turned left and started along a narrow gravel road toward, San Miguel de la Montaña.

Perched on a hillside above the town itself were tarpaper and metal shacks, the meager land surrounding each marked off by bundles of dried ocotillo branches serving as a fence.

At the center of the town were the mechanic's shop and the *gasolinera* Father Flannery had spoken of. A short distance beyond was the cantina. Along the street there was a *tienda,* where groceries were sold, and some sort of a barber shop. But the rest appeared to be abandoned and had fallen into disrepair. On the marquee of what had once been a small cinema, Jon saw the name *Mundo de Sueño*—Dream World. Across from the cantina was an outdoor market, empty now, except for chickens wandering among the stalls.

"I know this place," Emilio said. "Once, when the highway was closed, they detoured us through here. I even stopped to get a bite to eat at the cantina. My mistake. If chili is the special of the day, refuse it."

"Why?"

Emilio pointed to a pair of bony mongrels sleeping near the open door of the cantina. "See those dogs? When the cantina makes *chili con carne,* dogs like those are generally the *carne.* It keeps down the canine population."

"Thanks for the advice." Jon handed him the small black case. "By the way, would you give this back to Father Flannery? I've decided that I'm going to travel light."

"Are you really sure you want me to leave you in this place?" Emilio did not seem happy at the thought.

"Yes."

"Good luck, then." Emilio offered out his hand. "Call me as soon as you're back in the U.S."

"I will." Jon shook the hand and felt it tighten in his grasp. He stepped out of the truck.

Emilio pulled into the street, the truck stirring up a fine haze of dust as it turned around, and headed back toward the main road.

Jon started toward the door of the cantina. As he approached, one of the dogs lifted its head and stared at him with soulful eyes.

"Don't worry. I'm not having the chili," Jon assured it. He stepped through the open door.

The cantina was divided into two large rooms: a front room, which contained a bar and wooden tables and chairs, and a rear room, where laughter and the click of pool balls colliding could be heard. There was a door behind the bar from which smoke and cooking odors wafted.

Three young men in jeans and T-shirts faced the bar, each drinking a bottle of beer and talking quietly among themselves. The bartender, who was nowhere to be seen, was probably in the kitchen. Whatever he was cooking remained unidentifiable.

Jon sat at a table near the door and looked around the room. The walls were of a sickly yellow, aged by cigarette and cooking smoke. There were a few posters—one advertising a pre-Castro era bullfight in Havana, and another for a Mexican film that featured underclad and overbreasted women frolicking along a beach.

The door behind the bar opened and a man appeared carrying a plate. He set it down before one of the young men at the bar and said something in Spanish. The young man answered and began to eat.

Jon was about to signal when the bartender noticed him and came across the room in his direction.

"*Sí?*" the bartender inquired.

"*Cerveza,*" Jon said. "Beer."

"Tecate or Modelo?" the man said, asking for the brand.

"Tecate, *por favor.*"

The man nodded and returned to the bar. He found a bottle of Tecate, looked across the room at Jon again, and decided the Americano would also want a glass to drink it from. He brought the bottle and the glass, as well as a small bowl of pretzels, and set them on the table before Jon.

Jon looked up. "Javier," he said.

The bartended seemed not to understand.

"Javier," Jon said a second time. "Is he here? *¿Él está aquí?*"

Either the bartender still didn't comprehend him, or he was deciding what response to give. Finally, he turned and walked slowly toward the rear room of the cantina.

As he did, a pair of teenage girls came through the door to the street. One looked about sixteen; the other somewhat younger. The older girl's hair was a curious red ocher that suggested a bad henna rinse. The younger girl's was jet black and upswept in a beehive style that was certainly a wig. Their dresses, both bubble-gum pink, ended well above midthigh and displayed their shapely legs. Both wore open pumps with spike heels so tall their ankles wobbled slightly as they walked.

The girls stopped. They scanned the room, then whispered to each other, giggling. The older girl ambled toward the door leading to the pool room. As she entered it, cheers could be heard among the men. The younger girl kept her eye on Jon and walked toward him with a kind of rolling gait. She sat down next to him and smiled.

"*Buenas tardes, Padre.* You are American?" she asked in thickly accented English.

"Yes."

She put her fingers on his hand. "My name is Bianca. What's yours?"

"Father Nicholas Finch."

"And you are hot. Americans come from a cold country, so they get hotter than Mexicans." She stroked his hand and smiled. "But I am hot, too. Like you. Can I taste your beer?"

Not waiting for an answer, she picked up the bottle of Tecate, thrust the stem into her mouth, and drank. She removed the bottle, slowly ran her tongue around the top, and set it down.

"I speak English pretty good, yes?" she asked Jon.

"Yes."

"My mother worked in the house of an American in Cuernavaca. He was a teacher." She giggled again. "He taught my sister and me many things. So Father Nicholas Finch, how about we do some fun together, you and me?"

"No. I'm waiting for someone."

"*Rápido,*" she encouraged. "I live close on the hill."

"Scram!" a voice behind her demanded.

Jon looked up to see the bartender standing at the table. Beside him was a muscular young man. The bartender gestured to Bianca that she should leave.

Bianca rose, gave the bartender a gesture of her own, and headed to the room in back.

The bartender sat down opposite Jon. The young man took another chair, turned it around, and sat straddling it. He was wearing a T-shirt that said Planet Hollywood—New York. The sleeves of the T-shirt had been cut off, so as to accentuate his biceps.

"This is Javier," the bartender announced. "He does not speak English. I speak for him."

Javier said something to the bartender in Spanish, at the same time inclining his head toward Jon.

"Javier says he's never seen a priest in the cantina," the bartender translated. "He says sometimes we get tourists who are lost and can't find the main road. Are you lost?"

"In a sense," Jon said. "Tell him I'm looking for the road that leads to the United States."

The bartender translated for Javier. The young man listened and shrugged, then gave the bartender his reply.

"There are many roads that lead to the United States," the bartender told Jon. "The only road Javier knows is a toll road. He asks if you have money for the toll, or if you are a poor priest, like the rest."

"Tell him I have some money," Jon said. "If he helps me to take the road, how much is required?"

The bartender and Javier conversed rapidly. Javier turned back to Jon and held up four fingers.

"Four hundred dollars American," the bartender confirmed.

"Four hundred dollars is a lot," Jon said.

"Then you should find someone who knows a different road," the bartender said, not bothering to translate.

"*Sí. Cuatro,*" Javier said. Jon suspected the young man understood more English than he let on.

Jon reached into his visa case and below the level of the table withdrew some bills. He counted off four hundred-dollar bills, rolled them in his hand, and extended his hand across the table. Javier placed his own hand under Jon's and took the bills. He also counted them below the table.

"*¿ Habla español?*" Javier asked Jon directly.

Jon made a motion with his hand. "*Muy poco*. A little."

Javier grinned. He leaned across the table at Jon and jabbered something in Spanish.

The bartender also grinned. "Javier asks if you know what he just said."

"I haven't a clue," Jon admitted.

"He said there's an elephant in the toilet bowl wearing his mother's hat, which is made of butterflies."

Javier and the bartender laughed heartily.

"Tell Javier I want to know about the bus," Jon said, showing his impatience. He addressed Javier. "*El autobús a los estados únidos.*"

Javier hesitated.

"Tell him I just paid him four hundred dollars," Jon reminded the bartender. He looked at Javier again. *"El autobús."*

Javier shrugged, then said something to the bartender. The bartender nodded.

"Javier says the bus will be at the *gasolinera* at six," the bartender said. "There are others like you, going on the same road, already on the bus. When it leaves here, it will continue north, making stops along the way. A mile from the border is the town of Santa Valeria. You and the others will go into the bus station and wait. At ten o'clock, some men will approach. You will go with them. They will see to it you get across the border."

"Once we're across, then what?"

The question was put to Javier. The young man gave a short reply.

"Javier says once you're across, it's no concern of his. If you're murdered by American *bandidos,* that's your problem, not his."

"How comforting," Jon said.

Javier continued in Spanish to the bartender, who chuckled several times, then turned to Jon.

"You have three hours to wait until the bus arrives. Javier thinks you should make yourself comfortable. Have something to eat. Unfortunately, he says the town has few activities for tourists. No hotels; the cinema closed several years ago."

Javier passed on another suggestion. The bartender chuckled again. "He says, of course, you could spend those hours with Bianca and her sister in their trailer on the hill. For a little extra money, their mother will take part. It's a family business. When the town had a church, the priest used to make how should I say?— a pastoral visit to them every week, generally on Sundays after mass.''

"Thank Javier for his suggestions," Jon said. "But I'll find another way to spend my time. Is there anything worth seeing in the town at all?"

"Only the cemetery," the bartender said. "That should tell you something about this place."

"Sí. El cementerio," Javier agreed. *"Muy bonito."*

The young man stood. *"Buena suerte, Padre,"* he told Jon, and sauntered out of the cantina.

The bartender stood, as well. "Would you like something to eat?" he asked Jon. "The eggs are fresh."

"All right. Two eggs, scrambled. And some toast."

"Sí," the bartender said, and went in the direction of the kitchen.

A moment later, there was a burst of laughter from the room in back. Two couples came through the doorway: Bianca and her sister, accompanied by two men in their late fifties, both overweight and wearing polyester suits. One man had his arm around Bianca's waist. The other held the sister's hand, their fingers intertwined. As the four crossed the room, Jon noticed that the man who'd had his hand around Bianca's waist had lowered it, so that the hand now cupped her buttocks, fingers spread. Still laughing, the four of them stepped through the door into the street.

Jon sipped his beer. At last, his scrambled eggs arrived. Jon saw the yokes were nearly raw, as was a good bit of the white. The toast was warm, but smeared with some sort of viscous substance that smelled vaguely like an auto lubricant. Jon pushed the plate aside.

He finished his beer, put some pesos on the table, and left the cantina. Outside, the day had grown extremely hot. A gauze of high, thin clouds that had begun to move in from the west brought no relief. The air was motionless. Beside the door of the cantina, the dogs Jon had seen earlier were gone.

He walked the short distance to the *gasolinera*. Along the street, in front of it, was an unpainted wooden bench with a corrugated metal sheet above to provide shade. There were two gasoline pumps. In a shed behind them sat a man in overalls. He was watching Jon with an expression that looked more than just suspicious. It was menacing. His stare, combined with the noxious smell of the sulfurous Mexican gasoline, inclined Jon to continue on.

After walking for some minutes, Jon heard a pitiable sound: a harsh, discordant cry of pain. Glancing up a street, he noticed a young burro tethered to a cart. The harness had somehow produced an open, bleeding wound below the burro's eye. Each time the burro moved, the harness ring bit into the wound, making it bleed more. Suddenly the owner of the cart appeared. He shouted curses at the animal, slapped a whip across the burro's flank, and headed off.

Jon continued to walk on. But the image of the

burro lingered in his mind. More and more, he realized this was a place of cruelty and evil.

He had gone nearly to the outskirts of the town when he discovered the cemetery. Enclosing it was a wrought-iron fence, newly painted in white. Unlike the town itself, the cemetery was immaculately clean, attended to by caring hands. The gravel paths among the graves were freshly raked. Most of the wooden crosses on the graves had been adorned with artificial flowers of bright yellow, blue, and red. At one grave, the beatific figure of the Virgin of Guadelupe looked out from a stone grotto with a serene gaze. There was even an acacia tree that shaded a small iron bench.

Jon entered the cemetery and sat down on the bench. In the branches of the tree a pair of summer tanagers darted among the leaves, chirping as they flew.

It was then Jon heard a shuffling of feet.

Turning, he saw an elderly peasant woman entering along the path. In her arms she held bouquets of bougainvilleas.

She noticed Jon and stopped. She smiled. *"Buenas tardes, Padre,"* the old woman said.

"Buenas tardes." Jon returned the smile.

"Las flores para los muertos," she said, indicating the bouquets.

"Sí. Flores para los muertos." Flowers for the dead.

She continued to a grave that bore a tiny wooden cross. She knelt, placed a bouquet against it, crossed herself, and began to pray.

Observing her, Jon was reminded of the attitude toward death that many Mexicans shared. It combined grief, macabre humor, and pagan ritual with expressions of joy and festivity: one last fiesta for the dead before they journeyed to the afterlife.

The woman rose. Then, to Jon's surprise, she started toward him. Facing him, she drew a flower from the one of the bouquets she was carrying and held it out.

Her ink-black eyes bored into his. She placed the single flower in his hand, then turned again and walked away.

FOURTEEN

BLACK SMOKE hiccupped from the exhaust as the bus moved down the street in Jon's direction. It shuddered to a stop opposite the *gasolinera*.

The vehicle was obviously an ancient school bus, the yellow painted over with a pale blue. RÁPIDO AUTOBÚS it said along the side. Ironic, Jon thought, considering it was an hour late. Lashed to a roof rack were a number of cloth bundles and battered suitcases as well as two spare tires.

During the hours he had waited for the bus, Jon had disposed of his visa. It was a risk, but necessary for the story he would use to explain his presence in the country.

The bus sat idling. Finally, the doors swung open. Jon waited to see if any passengers were getting off. When none appeared, he climbed aboard.

"*¿Destino?*" the driver asked, without looking up.

"Santa Valeria," Jon said.

The driver told him the amount. Jon paid in pesos and started up the aisle toward the rear. There were about ten passengers. Most were men in their twenties and thirties, wearing canvas pants and T-shirts and holding knapsacks on their laps. There were two women: one old and quite fat, the other young and rather pretty. The man beside the young women had his arm around her shoulder in a proprietary way. Many of the men were smoking cigarettes or small cigars, and a miasma of smoke filled the interior of the bus.

Jon took an empty seat in the last row. Across the aisle from him was a wiry-looking young man in his twenties. Unlike the others, he was dressed in a white cowboy shirt with a snap front, open halfway down so that much of his chest hair was exposed. Instead of canvas shoes, he wore elaborately tooled cowboy boots with high Mexican-style heels that pointed his feet unnaturally downward at the toes. In one hand he held a Walkman cassette player. Jon could hear *ranchero* music seeping from around the earphones covering the young man's ears. As Jon sat down, the young man gave him a brief, friendly smile.

Jon took a deep breath—and wished he hadn't. In the row ahead of him, one man was eating tacos and fried potatoes from a bag. Another plucked serrano chilies from a can. The odor of food, as well as the cigar and cigarette smoke, mixing with the fumes from the bus exhaust that seeped up through the floor was sickening. How many hours he'd have to endure it, Jon didn't want to guess.

The doors of the bus closed, the gears whined, and the bus labored onto the road again.

The route it took as it moved north was far more primitive than the one he and Emilio had taken earlier. The land itself was like a moonscape—barren desert scrub with only a few hardscabble farms. Beside the road, Jon occasionally saw dead animals: dogs, goats, even a few burros that had ignored the horns of vehicles traveling the road.

The villages along the route looked almost as impoverished as San Miguel. Now and then, the bus stopped to pick up or discharge passengers. The old woman got off, her place taken by a drunken field worker, who immediately fell into a deep sleep. Otherwise, the passengers remained the same.

Jon closed his eyes; whatever rest he could get now he knew he'd need. Sleep, however, was impossible. Too many concerns had filled his mind.

From the seat across the aisle Jon heard the crinkle of newspaper. The aroma of fried chicken filled the air.

Jon opened his eyes to see the young man in the cowboy shirt eating chicken pieces from a newspaper that was spread out on his lap. The outline of the Walkman was visible inside the knapsack, which now sat at his feet. He noticed Jon and waved a chicken leg in his direction. *"¿Pollo?"* the young man asked him, offering the leg.

Jon suddenly realized how hungry he was. *"Gracias,"* he said, and took the leg.

"You are an American priest?" the young man asked.

"That's right."

"Me, I learn English from the tapes they send to me. Also, I see lots of American movies."

He stuck a chicken bone in the corner of his mouth

like a cigarette, Humphrey Bogart style. "'Here's looking at you, keed,'" he said. "What do you think?"

"Very good," Jon lied.

The young man beamed. "And this 'Come and gemmie, copper'...James Cagney."

"I guessed."

"Also Cleent Eastwood." A scowl followed. "'Come on, Buster—make my day.'"

"You've seen a lot of movies," Jon said.

The young man laughed. "Maybe someday I go to Hollywood and be a movie star. More chicken?" He held up the newspaper with a few unappetizing parts.

"No, thank you—" Jon started to add a name and realized he didn't know it.

"Hilario," the young man volunteered.

"I'm Father Finch."

"You are a tourist?"

"Not really."

"A *mojado* then? A wetback?" Hilario appeared amused.

"No," Jon told him. "But like some who cross into the United States, I must do it by unofficial means."

"Do you have papers? Visa?"

"It was lost."

"So you are like us," Hilario said. "We have no work papers for the places we are going. But work is waiting for us. Arizona, New Mexico, California, Idaho."

"Have you ever been caught crossing the border?"

"Many times. *La Migra,* the border cops, they catch

us and send us back. We wait a day or two, then try again. Once they caught me in Montana, working on a ranch, and flew me in an airplane to Mexico.'' He laughed. ''Best trip of my life.''

''Besides you, how many others are there on the bus?'' Jon asked.

Hilario peered forward. ''*Cuatro*. Four of us, plus the woman. Usually we are more.''

''Do you know all of them?''

''Yes, we have made many trips together,'' Hilario said. He pointed to three men sitting several rows ahead. The man near the window was smoking a cigarette and studying the ceiling of the bus. On the aisle was a young man wearing a straw hat with a red feather stuck in the band. The third man across the aisle no longer had his arm around the young woman's shoulder, but was using his hands to gesture as he talked with the man in the straw hat. For her part, the young woman paid them no attention. Instead, she stared out of the bus window at the growing darkness, her face impassive and unreadable.

''The man with the cigarette, his name is Ernesto. The other two are Jesús and José,'' Hilario explained. ''They're from my village. See the hat Jesús is wearing? He calls it his lucky hat. Each time he wears it, our crossing is successful. He is my friend. Also, José is my friend, but not as much.''

Jon indicated the young woman. ''Is that José's wife?''

Hilario shook his head and smiled. ''Gabriella wishes it. He gave her an engagement ring and promised to get married in America. But José already has two wives in two countries—one in Florida and one in Mazatlán. Gabriella knows this, but she goes with José anyway because of love. She thinks once she is married to him, he will divorce the others and love only her. He won't.''

He glanced at Jon. ''You are a priest. Maybe you should marry them right now. At least, pretend. It would make her feel better.''

''About the crossing,'' Jon said. ''Do you know the *coyotes*?''

''Some.'' Hilario shrugged. ''They change a lot. Most are very bad. But the police are worse.''

''What do you mean?''

''Did you see Ernesto's face? The scar? Once he was the most handsome in the village. All the women were in love with him. Then, last year, crossing at Nuevo Laredo, he was detained by the *judiciales*. They demanded money. If he paid them, they said they would let him go. He paid what he had. But it wasn't enough. So they slashed his face.''

''Have you ever heard of someone called The Hawk?'' Jon asked him casually.

Hilario's reaction was a quick shaking of the head. Too quick, Jon thought.

''No,'' the young man said. Another head shake. ''No.''

The bus continued on. Hilario offered Jon the remaining piece of chicken: a neck. When Jon declined, Hilario ate it himself.

Jon leaned back in his seat again. He had just closed

his eyes, when he felt the bus lurch slightly to the left. It was followed by a dull, rhythmic thumping from below. At the front of the bus, the driver pounded the dashboard with a fist and slowed the vehicle.

Hilario sighed. "Bad tire," he said to Jon. "Half the time I ride this bus a tire goes flat. Say a prayer to the Virgin, the replacement won't be just as bad."

"Tonight I pray for many things," Jon said. "I'll add it to the list."

THE CHANGING OF the tire took almost a half hour. After wrestling a spare from the roof of the bus, the driver and several of the men set the jack in place and began to lift the bus. When the jack proved faulty, two men went out into the desert. They returned fifteen minutes later carrying a thick branch from a mesquite tree. After raising the jack, they rammed the branch into the center of it to keep the jack from collapsing, while they removed the flat and substituted the spare tire. The operation took another fifteen minutes. Finally, the driver and the passengers climbed back aboard. The bus proceeded on.

Returning to his seat, Hilario yawned, clearly fatigued. He pulled the knapsack from the floor, placed it at the far end of the seat, and, using it as a pillow, lay down and went to sleep.

An hour passed. Most of the time, Jon stared out the window into the blackness of the night. Then, gradually, he saw a glow on the horizon. As if awakened by some inner signal, Hilario sat up and began strapping on his knapsack.

He looked across at Jon. "Santa Valeria," he said, pointing toward the glow. "The end of one journey and the beginning of another."

Entering the town, Jon saw it was larger than the villages through which the bus had passed. The buildings were mostly of two stories, some painted in vivid blues and reds. The bus station itself was a large, rectangular structure of sheet metal siding that resembled a warehouse. The bus came to a halt opposite a sign that said ENTRADA and waited while the passengers stepped off and went inside.

The interior was harshly lit by rows of fluorescent lights suspended from the ceiling, many of them flickering or dark. To one side, there was a food counter that was closed, another counter that sold bus tickets, also closed, and several vending machines against a wall. In the center, there were long benches, covered in maroon leatherette that was cracked or ripped in places, so that the stuffing emerged in little puffs of white. The linoleum floor, a mottled gray and brown, was strewn with cigarette butts, gum wrappers, and discarded ticket stubs.

Several of the benches were occupied by men asleep. All looked like farm workers. Hilario, Hilario's three friends, and Jon and Gabriella found empty benches and sat down. Jesús stretched his arms and yawned as well. He leaned back, pulled his lucky hat down over his eyes, and went to sleep.

The wall clock above the food counter showed 11:28.

"The *coyotes* were supposed to meet us," Hilario said, looking around.

"The bus was almost two hours late getting here," Jon reminded him. "Maybe they'll come back later."

"Maybe." Hilario slapped his hands on his knees, stood, and walked to the vending machines that stood against the wall.

Jon watched as he put coins into the machine and pulled down the lever. When nothing happened, Hilario began slamming a hand against the face of the machine.

Jon heard a noise near the entrance door. As he looked toward it, a dwarf appeared, limping on what seemed to be a homemade crutch. His features were Hispanic, but his skin was unnaturally white. Hobbling across the waiting room, he made little grunting noises as he moved.

He turned and started down the aisle between the sleeping men, glancing back and forth at them. None of the men stirred. In the dwarf's free hand, he clutched what looked like miniature postcards.

He made his way around to where Jon and the others were, going first to José and Gabriella. He stopped before them and held up the postcards for them to see. Gabriella gave a brief glance toward José. José nodded, dug into his knapsack, found some coins, and gave them to the dwarf. The dwarf handed a card to Gabriella. She read it and gave it to José. Next, the dwarf approached Ernesto and Jesús, who had awakened, and repeated the routine of the card. Each gave the dwarf some pesos and received a card in return.

The dwarf now took a sideways step, so that he stood facing Jon. He stared, producing small, contorted movements with his mouth, as if debating with himself whether the priest was worth a try. Apparently, he was. He held up a card a short distance from Jon's face. What Jon saw was a drawing of the Virgin Mary with her arms outstretched. Below her was the word *Sordomudo*. Deaf-mute.

When Jon hesitating in responding, the dwarf began making a high, whining sound and banging the tip of his crutch against the floor.

Jon decided it was simpler to buy a card than suffer the impatience of an angry dwarf. Like the others, he found some pesos in his pocket and dropped them into the dwarf's waiting hand.

The dwarf limped off across the room and disappeared into the night.

A moment later, Hilario returned, carrying a pack of gum. "I pulled the lever for a Baby Ruth bar," he said, "and got this." He sat down next to Jon and tore open the packet.

"You missed a visitor," Jon said.

"I saw. I'm glad," the young man said. *"Malo,"* he added, nodding toward the exit door through which the dwarf had gone. "Very bad, that dwarf."

"What do you mean?"

"When I was a child, there was a dwarf living in my village, deaf and dumb like him. My grandmother, she said if he came close to you and looked you in the eyes, bad luck would follow. I believed her."

A look of apprehension suddenly swept over Hilario's face. "It follows now. Look there."

He inclined his head in the direction of the entrance door. Through it, one after another, came four policemen in gray-green uniforms.

They stopped, their eyes scanning the occupants of the waiting room. Then they spoke rapidly among themselves.

"*Judiciales*," Hilario whispered, his voice edged with fear.

Moving as a group, the four walked slowly down the rows between the benches, prodding those asleep with leather truncheons. When the sleeping figure woke, they would jab him in the ribs and order him to stand. Once he was on his feet, they would demand his papers, examine them, and hand them back. If the subject sat again, they would insist he stand a second time. When he did, they would move on.

The officers conferred among themselves again. One gestured to the aisle where Jon and the others were. Watching them, Hilario lowered his head and pretended to be going through his knapsack. If he hoped to be unnoticed by the officers, it didn't work.

Two *judiciales* approached him. While one held the tip of a truncheon under Hilario's chin, the other waved him to his feet. When Hilario stood, they ignored him and turned to Gabriella and José instead. One policeman put a hand on Gabriella's shoulder, daring José to react. Except for a tightening of his jaw, José had the good sense to do nothing. Gabriella herself looked meekly at the officer in charge, as if to mollify any suspicions about them he might have.

The officer looked at each person in turn, then ordered everyone to stand. At once, Hilario began speaking rapidly in Spanish to the officer. From what Jon could make out, Hilario was telling the policeman that Jon was not a member of their group.

The officer listened. Then he looked at Jon and shook his head. He shot a thumb in the direction of the exit door. Accompanied by the officers, the six were led from the bus station and along the street. They stopped, finally, at a gray-painted stucco building. On the door was some sort of official seal.

The room to which they were escorted was dimly lit by a single fixture in the ceiling. The walls had long ago been painted white but had become stained by mildew, giving the surface the appearance of some nasty skin disease. Two of the officers immediately took positions on each side of the door.

Except for a wooden bench, there was no furniture. Gabriella and José were waved to the bench. Jon and Hilario stood, Ernesto and Jesús sat on the floor with their backs against the wall. In spite of what had occurred, Jesús was still wearing his lucky hat. If it, indeed, had psychic powers to assure good luck, it wasn't doing much for any one of them right now.

There was another door on the far side of the room. Behind it, Jon could hear the voice of a man speaking on the telephone. There was laughter. The word *pollos* was repeated several times.

The conversation ended. Moments later, the door

opened. Standing in the doorway, virtually filling the space, was a giant of a man weighing close to three hundred pounds. But what drew immediate attention was a malformation of the lower jaw that made his mouth extend to the center of his cheeks, displaying what looked like an unnatural number of teeth. When the mouth opened, it made Jon think of a shark. He wondered if they would be its prey. From the markings on his uniform, he was the senior officer.

The man scanned the room, his eyes falling, finally, on Jesús. He walked to Jesús, lifted the hat, and tossed it in a corner of the room. He nodded to the two other officers. Before Jesús could respond, the two had seized him by the arms and propelled him into the room beyond.

Hilario watched as the door closed. "The *comandante*," he said. "All the *mojados* know of him. They call him *La Boca*—The Mouth."

From the room, they could hear Jesús's voice crying out ("*¡Dios mio!*—*¡Ay, no!*—*¡Por favor!*"). His pleas were met with shouts, followed by a series of loud thumps that sounded like a butcher's mallet pounding meat.

At last, the door opened, and again, supported by two officers, Jesús was flung into the room. He landed at the feet of Gabriella and curled at once into a ball. Blood was coming from his nose and ears and he was drenched in sweat.

The *comandante* reappeared in the doorway. This time his eyes fixed on Gabriella.

"*La puta,*" he said to the officers. He grinned,

stepped to her, and said something to her in Spanish Jon didn't understand. One of the officers held Gabriella's arms behind her, while another laughed and put a hand inside her dress.

It was too much for José. He leapt at the officer. The others sprang at him and slammed him against a wall. One put a pistol to his head.

Gabriella shrieked. The *comandante* slapped her in the face.

"Leave them alone! Both of them!" Jon ordered. He went to Gabriella and put his arm around her. The girl now sobbed uncontrollably.

Except for the sounds of Gabriella's sobs, the room was absolutely still.

The *comandante* turned to Jon. Slowly he removed Jon's arm from Gabriella. "A gringo priest," he said. "What is you name, priest?"

"Father Finch."

"Like the bird? The finch?"

"Yes."

"The finch bird; he is small but full of courage. You are not small. But are you full of courage, too?"

"In the doing of God's work, I try to be," Jon said.

"Are you employed in God's work tonight?" the *comandante* asked. "We see."

He nodded to the officers. As with Jesús, they grabbed Jon by the arms and forcibly thrust him into the other room. The *comandante* shut the door.

Unlike the outer room, the walls were painted in a blue pastel. File cabinets stood against one side. There were two windows on which venetian blinds were drawn. Before them was a metal desk that would serve any government bureaucrat: In and Out trays holding printed forms, a blotter, a receptacle for pencils, and another holding paper clips. Also on the desk was a small picture in a Lucite frame of a smiling woman, with two children on her lap, a boy and a girl. On the wall opposite the desk were several plaques as well as framed photograph of the *comandante* shaking hands with a former president of Mexico.

In contrast to it all, a battered piano stool sat in the center of the room.

"Sit," the *comandante* ordered Jon.

Before Jon could respond, the two policeman and forced him down on the piano stool.

The *comandante* held an open hand in Jon's direction. "Papers, if you please."

"I don't have them."

"Why not?"

"They were burned."

The *comandante* grunted. "Oh? Who burned them?"

"I'm not sure."

"But you have suspicions," the man said. "Tell me your suspicions."

"They were burned by certain of the military," Jon said.

"Where?"

"Chiapas state."

Again, the *comandante* registered surprise. "Chiapas. Interesting. Explain."

"I'd been in Chiapas, working with the native people," Jon said. "My presence apparently displeased a local official of the government. One night men dressed as soldiers entered the house where I was a guest and set fire to it. Everything was burned, including most of my possessions and my documents. I'm sure they also would have killed me, if I hadn't escaped."

"What city were you in?" The *comandante* asked it casually. "San Cristobal, the capital?"

"San Cristobal isn't the capital of Chiapas," Jon said. "Tuxtla Gutiérrez is."

The *comandante* smiled. "Very good, priest. I play a little game with you."

"The truth is, I was mostly in the countryside," Jon told him.

"What part?"

"Near the Guatemalan border."

"I ask," the *comandante* said, "because I was born in Chiapas. A beautiful region."

"Yes, it is."

"However, the Zapatista guerillas are still active in the countryside and many priests are helping in their cause. Were you?"

"No."

"Then why are you now traveling with the *mojados?*"

"I wanted to get back to the United States."

"Why?"

"Because my work in Mexico is done."

"Indeed it is," the *comandante* said. "You and the other priests have planted foolish thoughts in people's

heads. That's why they fight against us. If it were up
to me, I would kill all of them. That is an ambitious
goal, I admit.''

He smiled down at Jon. ''But maybe I will start with
you.''

He grabbed Jon's shoulders, spinning him around.
''Put your hands behind your back.''

Jon did as he was told. Handcuffs were immediately
clamped around his wrists. He was spun again, so that
he faced the officer once more.

In the *comandante*'s hand was a small canister. He
held it up. ''Do you know what is in this?''

''No.''

''It is the substance Mace,'' the *comandante* said.
''It is used to subdue criminals. But sprayed directly
down the throat, it gives great pain. Not only is the
subject unable to cry out, but he—''

There was a sharp knock at the door. The *comandante* looked annoyed. He signaled to one of the policeman. The officer stepped from the room.

He returned almost at once and whispered to the
comandante. The man nodded, glanced momentarily
at Jon, and spoke quickly to the other officer. The
officer stepped behind Jon and unlocked the handcuffs.

''You are free to go,'' the *comandante* told Jon,
obviously displeased to be saying it. ''You'll find your
friends awaiting you outside.''

The door to the outer room was opened and Jon
was pushed from the *comandante*'s office.

Standing in the outer room, Jon discovered it was
empty. The door leading to the corridor was open. Re-

tracing his steps through the building, he found a door that said *Salida* and walked through it. He was in an alleyway beside the building. Going to the street, he saw a pickup truck parked at the front entrance. Hilario and some of the other men were leaning against the rear bumper. In the open bed of the truck, Gabriella was bending over the limp form of Jesús, dabbing at his forehead with a piece of fabric from his shirt.

Hilario saw Jon and waved excitedly. "Over here, Father! Come to the truck. Get in!"

Jon went to it. Hilario, Ernesto, and José climbed into the back. They held out their hands and helped Jon aboard.

"We were afraid *La Boca* would kill you," Hilario said. "Thank God you're all right."

"I think God had some help," Jon told him. "What happened?"

"There was a mixup. A mistake," Hilario explained. "The *coyotes* came to the bus station at the time we should have been there. They didn't know we would be late. When they didn't find us there, they left. Even so, they came back later and were told we had been taken by the *judiciales*. In Santa Valeria, there is a new man who gives orders to the *coyotes* now. When he discovered what had happened, he asked *La Boca* to release us and, of course, paid a big bribe."

Ernesto held up Jesús's straw hat. Hilario saw it and laughed. "Before we left, Ernesto also picked up the lucky hat. I guess it's helping us at that."

Suddenly the front door of the police station opened and a figure began walking toward the truck.

"That's him," Hilario said, whispering. "The man who got us free. He is our savior."

The man approached the truck and opened the passenger door of the cab. Momentarily, in the dim light of the cab's interior, Jon saw their savior's face.

It was Victor.

FIFTEEN

THE TRUCK MOVED rapidly along the street, rumbling over potholes, as it gained speed. Jon and the others sat in the back of the pickup, holding onto the side rails, while Jesús lay curled in a corner. With every bump, the young man groaned.

The lights of Santa Valeria were soon behind them, leaving little more than a faint residue of yellow against the blackness of the night. Ahead, Jon could see nothing.

He knew he had to make a plan. And soon. Of one thing he was certain: It was necessary that he cross the border without Victor recognizing him. Was it possible? Victor had lost the opportunity to kill Jon once. He wouldn't let a second chance go by.

Jon thought momentarily of jumping from the vehicle. But the truck was traveling too fast. Even if it slowed, what then? Would he be able to cross the border on his own? And if he did, he would be carrying no food or water. In open desert, under rising temperatures, he could become delirious and die.

The groans of Jesús became louder. The truck was hurrying along a rough section of road, and the young man's head struck the bed of the truck with every jolt.

Gabriella went to him and cradled his head in her hands.

Jon knelt beside her and looked over at Hilario. "Give me your knapsack. Jesús needs a pillow for his head."

Hilario handed it across. Gently Gabriella lifted Jesús's head, and Jon placed the knapsack under it. The rough fabric of the knapsack wasn't ideal, but it provided a sufficient cushion. As Jon adjusted it, he saw Jesús's lucky hat lying beside him. The red feather was gone.

It gave Jon an idea. He picked it up. Blood covered the lining and the inside band.

"Do you think Jesús would mind if I wore his hat awhile?" Jon asked Hilario.

"It would hurt his head too much if he tried," Hilario said.

Jon placed the hat on his head. Although a size smaller than his own, it might serve the purpose he had in mind.

The pickup slowed and the ride became surprisingly smooth and straight. Leaning forward, Jon saw in the headlights that they were speeding along a stretch of level ground, too broad to be a road.

"This was once a landing strip for drug planes," Hilario explained. "They would take off from here and fly very low across the border. Once in Arizona, they would find another secret strip like this one, drop their cargo, and fly back."

"Is it still used?"

"No," the young man said. "The drug gangs

change them all the time. The authorities plan raids to catch the couriers. But the gangs are warned well in advance by the *judiciales*. So when the raids occur, they find only empty desert, that is all. No couriers, no planes, no drugs.''

"It's being used for something now," Jon said. "Look there."

He pointed in the direction that the truck was traveling. In the distance, a pair of lights blinked on and off. "It looks like somebody is signaling us to stop."

Hilario said nothing, but his face went tight.

The blinking continued, growing brighter, as the pickup truck approached.

"Who do you suppose they are?" Jon wondered. "More *judiciales?*"

"Maybe," Hilario said. "Some, even if they've been paid off, send men out along the route to shake down the *coyotes*. These, I think are not police. They're robbers."

"What do we do?"

"Stay down," Hilario advised him. "Out of sight if possible, and if they come to you, do what they say. Let the driver and the man with him in the cab take care of it."

Heeding his own advice, Hilario squatted on the bed of the truck, trying to make himself as inconspicuous as possible. The others did the same, including Jon.

Directly ahead, visible now in the truck's headlights, was an old Buick sedan, gray in color with its grille missing. The car's headlights blinked one final time, then dimmed.

The doors of the Buick opened and two men stepped out. *"Buenas noches,"* one called out. Both men wore the uniforms of the *judiciales*. But unlike those in Santa Valeria, they wore bandoliers of cartridges across their chests.

"Bandidos dressed like the police," Hilario whispered. "They'll try to make a deal with our driver and the other man to rob us and share what what's taken: money, jewelry, anything of value we have. If the men refuse, the *bandidos* will kill them anyway and rob us then. Either way, it's very bad."

Leaving the engine idling, the driver of the pickup slowly climbed out of the cab. Approaching the two men, he raised a hand, as if in greeting. Several yards from them, he stepped slightly to one side, out of the beam of the truck's headlights.

The three men spoke hastily in Spanish, the two in uniform gesturing in the direction of the truck.

"No, no," Jon heard the driver say.

As the driver and one of the men continued their animated conversation, the other began walking toward the truck. Fifteen feet away, a hand reached to the holster at his belt.

Suddenly a shotgun blast exploded from the right side of the cab. It catapulted the man backward onto the dirt, his face blown away, his upper body instantly a bloody mass.

A second blast struck the other, as he rushed to aid his partner. The impact knocked him back against the left front fender of the Buick. Then gradually, almost peacefully, he slipped down along the fender to the ground.

The driver of the pickup truck stepped into the light again. Assured that both were dead, he removed the pistols from their holsters and started back to the truck.

He flashed a thumbs-up sign, then climbed into the cab and threw the truck in gear. The truck drove on.

Almost at once, they began moving over rough terrain again. Except for Jesús, the others sat up and took hold of the side rails.

Then, unexpectedly, the pickup slowed and made a wide U-turn. Looking, Jon saw they were at the edge of an arroyo. The driver turned off the engine. The lights died.

In the darkness, Victor and the driver left the cab. Victor switched on a flashlight, which he directed at the ground. He turned and shouted several commands in Spanish to those in the rear of the truck.

"He wants us to get out of the truck and follow him," Hilario told Jon.

"I'll go behind you," Jon said. He pulled Jesús's hat forward and down, hoping to conceal as much of his face as possible, and joined Hilario and Ernesto, jumping to the ground. Meanwhile, José and Gabriella were holding Jesús on each side, as he eased his body down over the edge.

After more commands from Victor, they began walking. Victor and the driver, whose name, Jon learned, was Ramón, led the way. They descended into the arroyo. Victor kept the flashlight focused downward, sweeping it back and forth to check for hazards in their path. After walking several hundred yards along the arroyo, they climbed a steep bank.

They'd gone only a dozen yards when Ernesto cried out and fell to the ground. Victor spun around and shined the light at him. Ernesto had removed his sandal and sat rubbing his right foot. Long cactus needles were embedded in the skin.

The group gathered around him, with the exception of Jon, who stayed in the shadows looking on.

Victor cursed: It was obvious he wasn't pleased to have the trip delayed again. While Ernesto grimaced, trying to dislodge the needles, José found two small rocks and, using them like pincers, also attempted to remove the spines. The wounds they left were raw and ugly, as if barbed wire had been wrapped around Ernesto's foot.

Finally, José opened the satchel he'd been carrying, pulled out a plastic bottle, and poured water over the wounds. It was a considerable sacrifice. If they should be forced to walk far in the desert during the day, they would need all the water that they had.

On Victor's orders, Ernesto was helped to his feet. Gingerly he put on his sandal, grunting and clenching his jaw as he did. The group began to walk again. As before, Jon fell to the back of the line, joining Hilario.

"Poor Ernesto," Hilaraio said in a low voice. "It was a cholla he stepped on. Jumping cactus, they are called. Touch them and the spines seem to leap into your skin. They stick to anything. But lots of other things can hurt you in the desert at night: tarantulas, snakes, scorpions. Step on them when they are sleeping, they will let you know."

The terrain became more rugged. Now and then they stumbled in the thick scrub grass or tripped on fallen branches from ocotillo and mesquite. Each time Victor shouted, the person who had fallen rose again, and they walked on.

They had struggled up a steep incline, when Victor abruptly raised a hand. They stopped. He aimed the flashlight to his left. In the light they saw the hulk of an abandoned car. How it got there was a mystery. Its hood was gone. The tires had been stripped, along with the doors, bumpers, steering wheel, front and back seats, and whatever working parts the car once had. Like other desert carrion, it had been picked clean.

Victor and Ramon spoke briefly. Jon wondered if the derelict car served as some sort of a marker. When Victor swung the flashlight in the opposite direction, Jon knew he was right.

Illuminated by the beam was a wall of metal stretching off into the darkness.

"That's the border?" Jon asked Hilario.

"*La Frontera. Sí,*" he said.

On Victor's instructions, Ramón walked forward and stood facing it. The fence looked to be about twelve feet high. It was built of interlocking metal plates, with protruding horizontal ridges every several feet: perfect for providing foot-and handholds to the climber. Jon had imagined that the boundary separating Mexico and the United States was something far more formidable: electrified, perhaps, and surrounded by barbed wire. This fence, on the other hand, presented almost no deterrent to anyone with the determination and ability to climb it. Max Montoya's description had been right. She'd called it the Tortilla Curtain—hardly an intimidating image to anyone confronting it.

Quickly, Victor and Ramón scaled it, swinging their legs over the top and jumping down the other side. Gabriella and José followed, while with Ernesto's help, Jesús was moving stiffly upward just behind them.

"Doesn't the Border Patrol have infrared cameras near the wall to spot the climbers?" Jon asked Hilario.

"Many places they do," Hilario said. "But most times people cross over and are met by *coyotes* on the other side before *La Migra* can send officers." He laughed. "All they're left with are fuzzy pictures of people climbing, jumping down, and running off into the dark."

Ernesto and Jesús went over the top, followed by Hilario and Jon. A few feet from the ground, both jumped to the soft earth.

Hilario grinned. "Welcome to America, Father Finch. You are safe now."

"*¡Luz!*" someone shouted, pointing.

The others turned. A hundred yards away they saw the flickering red-orange flames of a bonfire.

"Those must be the *coyotes* who will take us north," Hilario said.

"What about the two who brought us across?" Jon asked him.

"They'll go back to Mexico. Each group of *coyotes* has his territory. There is an understanding," Hilario went on. "Mexican *coyotes* don't operate in the U.S., and those who are here don't cross into Mexico."

"What will happen now?"

"These two will deliver us to the *coyotes* waiting by the fire. Then they will return the way they came."

Jon felt a sense of hope. He had come this far without being recognized by Victor. Only a short time remained before Victor and Ramón handed them over to their new escorts and left.

But instead of urging them in the direction of the fire, Victor abruptly began shouting orders to the group in Spanish. At once, people sat down on the ground.

"He wants us to sit. Do it quickly," Hilario said in a low voice.

"Why?"

"We're being robbed."

Victor drew a pistol and held it toward the group, making certain that each person saw it. Satisfied they had, he aimed it at José, who was seated nearest him.

"*Prisa,*" Victor told José.

Hands trembling, José dug into his pockets and pulled out what cash he had. Ramón, who was standing next to Victor, took a red bandanna from a rear pocket of his jeans, and fashioned it into a makeshift bag. Victor passed along the cash José had given him, and Ramón placed it in the bandanna. Victor now pointed the pistol at José's feet. Unlike the others, who were wearing sandals, José had what looked like a new pair of Adidas running shoes.

"*Los zapatos,*" Victor said, waving the pistol.

"*¿Mis zapatos?*"

Victor fired a shot into the sand between José's feet, barely missing the left big toe.

His hands shaking again, José fumbled to undo the laces. He stripped off the shoes and set them on the ground. He looked up at Victor, pleading.

"*Los zapatos,*" Victor told him. "*Dentro.*"

When José didn't move, Victor aimed the pistol at the man's groin. José dug into the shoes at once. From each, he produced a quantity of U.S. hundred-dollar bills. Victor took them and stuffed them in Ramón's bandanna. Still trembling, José picked up his running shoes to put them on.

"*Uno momento,*" Victor said. From his right foot, he took off the scruffy loafer he'd been wearing, grabbed the shoe in José's hand, and compared the two. The loafer and the Adidas running shoe were the same size.

"*Bueno,*" Victor said. He removed the remaining loafer he was wearing. He slipped the running shoe onto his foot, took the other from José, and put it on as well. He smiled. "*Gracias,*" he told José, and tossed the loafers off into the dark.

He and Ramon now moved to Gabriella. For several silent moments Victor looked at her, as if deciding what to do. Then he touched the barrel of the pistol to the engagement ring on her left hand and tapped it with the gun.

Gabriella appeared stricken. *"Oh, no, señor,"* she begged Victor. *"Por favor."*

She began to shake. José put his arm around her and spoke softly. Gabriella slid off the ring and held it up. Victor took it and put it in his pocket.

Next, he stepped to Jesús and shined the flashlight in his face. In the harsh glare from it, the young man's wounds were a ghastly sight. Victor decided it wasn't worth the effort and approached Ernesto.

Hilario would follow, that was certain. Jon would be last, that was certain, too. There was no way of escaping Victor now.

Victor took the money Hilario offered him and passed it to Ramón.

At last, Victor stood in front of Jon. Keeping his head down, as if submissively, Jon offered up what cash he had.

But instead of extracting the money from Jon's out-stretched hand, Victor seized him by the wrist and held the flashlight beam against it.

"Pálido," he observed. "White skin. Are you An-glo?"

"Yes," Jon said, keeping his head down.

Victor snatched the hat and tossed it aside. "Raise your head. I want to see your face."

Jon did as Victor ordered. The other shined the light into his eyes.

"So…" Victor said. "You are a man of many oc-cupations. When we met, you said you were a rancher.

Now you are a priest. I'll tell you what you are: a cop. A cop pretending he is one of the *mojados*."

Victor spoke quickly to Ramón. Ramón placed the bandanna on the ground and opened it. As Ramón watched, Victor divided up the cash, pocketing his portion, and leaving the remainder for Ramón.

Then Victor shined the flashlight at the border fence and issued orders to Ramón. When Ramón started to object, Victor raised the pistol casually.

"Okay," Ramón said to him. He was visibly unhappy with the instructions he'd been given. Then, as Victor and the others watched, he turned and trudged back in the direction of the fence.

Victor swung the light around again and gave a sharp command. At once, the group began to rise.

"Walk ahead of me by three steps," he said to Jon. "I'll be behind you with the gun. The rest will go in front of us."

More commands and the group slowly moved forward single file toward the bonfire. As they walked, Jon saw Hilario glance back at him. The young man looked terrified.

The three men who stood around the fire greeted Victor as the group arrived. Victor raised a hand briefly. Of the men, two were Hispanic; the third, an Indian. All were dressed in dark sweatshirts and jeans. In the firelight, Jon saw the Indian's face was deeply pockmarked. On his head he wore a baseball cap with the logo of the Arizona Diamondbacks. A cigarette hung loosely from his lips. The Hispanics held shotguns at their sides. A short distance away, Jon noticed two pickup trucks.

"We saw the flashlights and expected you sooner," one of the young men said. He smiled. "What were you doing, plucking chickens?"

"What happened to Ramón?" the Indian asked Victor.

"I sent him home."

"And you? Are you going home?" the Indian said.

"I decided to come back to the U.S. and stay awhile," Victor told him.

"Why?"

"Mexican food doesn't agree with me."

The men laughed.

"Also," Victor said, "I have a gift for *El Halcón*."

"What is it?" one of the men said.

Victor looked at Jon.

"A priest," he said.

SIXTEEN

VICTOR WAVED WITH both hands at the trucks. *"¡Los camióens! i Los camióens!"* he shouted.

Hilario and the others began heading toward the pickup trucks, where the Hispanics were lowering the tailgates. Jon started to follow them.

"Not you." Victor grabbed his arm. "You ride with me."

Still gripping his arm, Victor directed him toward the cab of the second truck and opened the passenger door. "Get in. Sit in the middle," Victor instructed him. "Put both hands on the dashboard where I can see them."

As he climbed into the truck, Jon saw Hilario, José, and Gabriella standing in the bed of the other truck. The two Hispanics were entering the cab. Jon looked at the rearview mirror of his truck and saw Ernesto helping Jesús over the tailgate. The cab itself reeked of tobacco smoke and alcohol. A packet of cigarettes lay on the dashboard in front of the steering wheel.

Victor sat down next to Jon, closed the door, and locked it. The Indian hoisted himself into the driver's seat. He put the cigarette pack to his mouth, extracted a cigarette with his lips; and lit it. With Victor at his right and the Indian's thigh pressed against him on the left, Jon tried to adjust himself on the seat. He felt Victor's pistol in his ribs.

"Stay as you are," Victor ordered him.

The headlights of the other truck flashed on. The truck made a long arc and started off. The Indian did the same, staying at a distance from the truck ahead, as they traveled what seemed to be a meandering dirt road.

No one spoke. The Indian finished his cigarette, tossed the butt out the window, and immediately lit another.

As they rounded a sharp curve, Jon moved a hand instinctively to brace himself. Again he felt the jab of Victor's pistol at his side.

"Hands on the dashboard," Victor snapped.

The pickup trucks turned onto a paved highway. Jon had no sense of what direction they were heading, except that they were well away from the border. The road signs were now shaped like arrowheads, an indication they had entered an Indian reservation, probably that of the Papago.

And they were climbing. Instead of scrubgrass, cactus, and mesquite, they were ascending among chaparral and juniper. Remembering a field trip he'd taken early in his visit, Jon guessed they were crossing the Baboquivari Mountains that formed the southeast border of the reservation. Beyond the mountains, they descended into a high valley. East of it the terrain began to rise again. As they drove on, the headlights of the pickup trucks revealed steep-sided canyons and dense brush. Here and there was the evidence of ruined buildings and wooden towers and narrow, weed-covered tracks that suggested long-abandoned mines.

"An interesting area," Victor observed, sounding like a tour guide. "We are in another part of the national forest. Along the way you will see ghost towns and played-out mines that once were rich with gold, silver, zinc, and copper. Places like Ruby and Hank and Yank Spring." He laughed. "You must visit them sometime," he advised Jon.

"Thanks for suggesting it," Jon said. "I'll try."

"Now," Victor went on, "tell me about your friends: the other cops. Tell me about the woman who saved your life at the museum. I know she is a cop, too. What's she like in bed?"

"I wouldn't know."

"Ho, ho—I think so." Victor grinned. "You and she—*coito*, yes?"

Jon ignored the question.

"If not, too bad for you. She's pretty. And a widow. Probably hot and very lonely since her husband died. You knew him, maybe. He was a *pinche* cop like you."

"I know he died. That's all," Jon said.

"But do you know *why* he died?" asked Victor. "It was because we think he knew the name."

"What name?"

"The name of *El Halcón. El Halcón* could not allow that. So the cop is killed."

"Were you the one who killed him?"

"No, but it was me who drove the car," Victor said almost proudly.

"Who shot him?"

"You'll meet him soon." The other paused. "Also, you will meet *El Halcón.*"

Abruptly they descended into a wide canyon. In spite of the rocky upthrusts of the canyon walls, the road was smooth and reasonably straight. The canyon gave way to undulating hills, crisscrossed by shallow mountain streams. Each time the trucks reduced their speed and forged the swiftly moving current, sheets of water splashing at their wheels.

They had climbed a slight embankment, when Jon saw the beginnings of a sturdy chain-link fence, surmounted by barbed wire. Attached to the fencing was a NO TRESPASSING sign. The sign was repeated every hundred feet.

"So tonight it's Oro Rojo?" Victor asked the Indian.

The Indian nodded without turning his head.

Jon remembered Max had mentioned several locations where the *coyotes* sometimes brought their charges. One was Monte Dulce; the another, Kyler's Pass. The third was a place called Oro Rojo. The name in Spanish meant red gold, most likely for the veins of reddish ore found there. But considering the money—and often the blood—the smugglers extracted from their victims, it had a meaning that was far more sinister.

The pickup driven by the two Hispanics slowed and stopped before a set of open gates. The Indian did the same. Beyond them, Jon could see evidence of what was a deserted mining town. Because the land was protected by the fence and most likely in private hands, it hadn't fallen victim to the vandals and souvenir hunters who had laid waste to so many ghost towns in the West.

The trucks drove through the gates. Now, Jon could make out low buildings, some of wood, the rest adobe. Near one small wood-frame building, standing timbers remained of what had been the headframe of a mine, a pyramidlike structure from which ore buckets were lowered and raised. The road continued past a cemetery adjacent to a church. The church was without a steeple; spaces where the doors and windows once had been gaped vacantly. Beyond was a crumbling building that may have been a schoolhouse. In front of it, one end of a child's seesaw rose among the weeds.

A half-mile ahead, the center of the town appeared. More wooden buildings, some of several stories, stretched along both sides of the wide street. A few bore signs, the names of which were barely visible. In the headlights from the trucks, Jon identified the assayer's office, the livery and blacksmith shop, and the depot for the Tucson-Nogales Overland Stage Company. The largest of the buildings had no signs. But from the look of it, Jon suspected it had served as the town's hotel, gambling hall, and saloon. In the center, facing out onto the boardwalk separating it from the street, was a large, open doorway.

The pickup trucks pulled up in front of it and turned off their engines.

Victor opened the door of the cab and glanced at Jon. "Keep your hands on the dashboard."

"What if he tries to escape?" the Indian asked.

"Shoot him."

"I don't have a gun," the Indian said.

"You're always supposed to carry one," Victor told him, irked.

"I forgot," the Indian said.

Victor started around the front of the truck. *"Pinche Indio,"* he said to himself. He handed his pistol to the Indian through the driver's window.

"Make sure you know which end the bullet comes out," Victor said.

The Indian took the pistol, saying nothing.

Victor turned and walked in the direction of the building. Standing on the boardwalk under an overhanging porch, he peered in through the entranceway. If he was anticipating a response from someone inside, none came.

He took a breath, then spat into the street and peered again. Nothing. He walked along the boardwalk to a window, cupped his hands, and put his face up to the opening. Still, there was no sign, no signal, anyone was there. In the darkness, Jon heard Victor mutter a *"Mierde."*

A minute passed.

Then, just as Victor turned again and began walking toward the truck, there was a sound. It was a high, shrill *pweee,* repeated several times.

Victor froze. He stepped to the entranceway, took another breath, and responded with a clucking sound.

"I'm sorry we're late," Victor said into the dark, empty room. "There was some trouble. It delayed us."

"Where are Felipe and Miguel?" someone inside the room asked.

Jon strained to hear the voice. It sounded Hispanic. He remembered hearing it somewhere before, but he couldn't identify the speaker.

"They're in the cab of the first truck," Victor said. "I told them I would speak for them."

There was whispered conversation with a second person in the darkened room.

"Is it you, Victor?" the Hispanic voice asked at last. It was as if he were relaying the other person's words.

"Yes," Victor said.

"Why are you here? You were supposed to stay in Mexico."

"Ramón was drunk," Victor said. "I couldn't let the *pollos* come alone. Also, I want to return to the United States. I think it's safe."

There was more conversation from inside the room. Then a figure appeared in the doorway. From where Jon sat, he couldn't see the face.

"You said you had trouble tonight," the figure added, still speaking with a Hispanic inflection to the words. "What trouble?"

"There was a problem in Santa Valeria," Victor said. "The bus was late in getting there. When we came the first time, the *pollos* weren't there. When we went back a second time, we heard *La Boca* and the *judiciales* had detained them. I was required to pay a lot of money for their release. But there's more I have to tell.''

"What else?''

"Before we crossed, *bandidos* stopped us,'' Victor said. "They tried to rob us.''

"Did they?''

"No. I shot them.''

There was a lengthy pause. "How many *pollos* do you have?'' the person in the doorway asked.

"In all, there's five,'' Victor said. "And someone else. A *gringo,* who I think—''

"He wants the *pollos* to get out of the trucks,'' the other said. "He wants them on the street where he can see them.''

Victor called to the two young men from the first truck, who were now standing on the street next to their vehicle. At once, the two began calling to Hilario and the others in both trucks to climb down. Quickly, all complied, including Jesús, who this time managed on his own.

Suddenly a light shone through the window of the room, striking the faces of the people where they stood. Some covered their eyes with their hands.

"Hands down,'' the figure in the doorway said.

The hands were lowered and all stared toward the building as the beam of the light slowly passed across their faces. When it reached Jesús, it stopped. Jon heard a voice from inside the room.

"That one,'' the figure asked. "He wants to know what happened to his face.''

"The man was beaten by *La Boca*," Victor said.

The light continued on, ending on the face of Gabriella. Her eyes were shut and her head bowed.

Again, a muffled voice from the room.

"Her," the man in the doorway said to Victor. "*El Halcón* asks if she was touched by anyone."

"Not that I know of," Victor said.

"What about you?" said the man. "He's heard things about you he doesn't like."

"I didn't touch her," Victor assured him.

The light inside the room went out.

"All right," the man said. "Tell them they can get back in the trucks. They can be taken to the house in Tucson."

Jon could feel the relief among the group. Even the Indian beside him grunted. The two other *coyotes*, Felipe and Miguel, again shouted commands, and Hilario and the rest hurriedly began climbing into the trucks.

"*Gracias,*" Victor said. "I'll tell the Indian I'll join him a few minutes." He started for the trucks.

"No. You're staying here," the figure in the doorway said.

Victor turned, surprised. "But I thought—"

"*El Halcón* wants you to stay. He says he and you must talk."

"Can't we talk in Tucson?" Victor sounded apprehensive.

From inside the darkened room, Jon heard an immediate response.

"He says it's necessary that you talk tonight."

Victor drew in a breath. "Fine. Okay. But tell him I have something to give him that will please him."

"What is it?"

"Call it a gift."

"What kind of gift?"

"An undercover cop, who was crossing with the *pollos.*"

"A border cop?" the figure asked.

"Yes," said Victor. "Pretending he's a priest."

Jon closed his eyes. The thing he feared the most was happening.

"*¿La Migra?*" asked the figure. "Are you sure?"

"I'm sure. He was the one who came to the used car lot," Victor said. "The same one I was with in the Desert Museum, when the woman cop showed up."

"Where is he?"

"In the truck with the Indian. I gave the Indian my gun."

"That was stupid."

"The Indian forgot his," Victor explained.

"Bring in this cop, so we can see him," said the figure.

"With my pleasure," Victor said.

He walked to the truck where Jon and the Indian sat and wrenched open the door. "Come on, cop. Into the building. Some people want to meet you."

Jon swung his legs over and stepped out of the cab.

Victor leaned in and spoke to the Indian. "You. Wait. I'll be right back." He looked over at Felipe and Miguel in the other truck. "You, too. Wait here."

Victor turned to Jon. "Let's go."

Jon moved toward the building. Out of the corner of his eye, he saw those in the back of the trucks watching him. Gabriella crossed herself.

With Victor at his back, Jon entered the large room. At the far end, a broad stairway led up to an overhanging balcony. The room itself was empty, except for a long wooden table placed beneath the balcony. Behind it, deep in shadows, sat a man. Two empty chairs faced him.

To the right of the table stood a young man. He appeared to be in his late teens. Holding an automatic rifle, he was chewing at a piece of gum with manic energy, his jaw working constantly from side to side.

But it was the man standing to the left of the table whom Jon looked at now. He was the figure in the doorway to whom Victor had spoken, the Hispanic voice Jon had heard. The man was Agent Martinez. Instead of his uniform, he was dressed in a dark sweatshirt and jeans.

Martinez indicated the two chairs facing the table. "Sit there. Both of you. Otherwise, Placido will get nervous and shoot."

He nodded toward the young man with the gun. Placido seemed anything but placid. The gum chewing became faster and Placido's hand ran a hand up and down the barrel of the gun.

Suddenly the man sitting opposite them at the table laughed. The laughter grew, then stopped. "This is your policeman?" he asked Victor.

"Yes."

The man stood up and leaned forward.

Jon saw Stuart Van Dine's face for the first time.

"You're a fool, Victor," Van Dine said. He was dressed in dark slacks. A windbreaker covered much of a dark shirt.

"He's not a cop or a priest, either," Van Dine said, with obvious disgust.

"He acted like a cop the first time I met him."

"And still, you arranged to meet him later at the museum."

"Yes, but he—"

"Let me ask you, Victor. What if he had been a cop, what then? What would you have done? By meeting him, weren't you exposing yourself to further risk?"

"I thought he might be working on his own, the way that woman's husband was," Victor insisted. "I planned to kill him later on. I wasn't counting on the woman being there."

"Was that your plan?" Van Dine asked. "Or was it to keep the money for yourself?"

"No, No." Victor shook his head. "Whatever he paid me I would have given it to you."

"Would you, Victor?"

"Yes, yes, I would."

"After your meeting with him was interrupted, what did you do?"

"You know what I did," Victor said. "I fled to Mexico. Those were your orders."

"That's right," Van Dine agreed. "And the other

orders that I gave you? Do you remember what they were?"

"I think—"

"Do you, Victor?"

"Yes."

"Tell me."

There was a short intake of breath. Jon could hear Victor wet his lips. "Your orders were for me to stay in Mexico and not return to the United States."

"And tonight you disobeyed me."

"I had no choice," Victor said at once. "I told you, Ramón was too drunk to take the *pollos* across. I did it in his place."

"We contacted Ramón a short time ago," Van Dine told him. "He didn't sound drunk. He said you sent him back. You ordered him."

"Ramón seemed drunk to me, I thought—"

"He said you also robbed the *pollos*. Is that true?"

"No. Absolutely not. Ramón did."

"Stand up," Van Dine ordered.

Victor stood.

"Empty your pockets."

Victor hesitated. "I carried extra cash tonight," he insisted. "After I paid *La Boca,* I still had some."

"Empty them, and put what's in them on the table," Van Dine said. "Do it or Placido will take off your pants and do it for you."

Placido grinned.

Hastily Victor thrust his hands into his pockets. From them he withdrew a quantity of crumpled bills, as well as several gold chains, a wristwatch, and a small cross set with precious stones. As one of the bills uncurled, Gabriella's engagement ring slid onto the table.

Van Dine reached out and took the ring. He held it up. "Is this ring also yours?"

"Yes."

"Put it on." He handed it to Victor.

Victor's hands began to shake. Slowly he slipped it over his ring finger. It stopped at the first knuckle. He tried the little finger. It made it to the second knuckle and no further.

"Give me the ring," Van Dine said.

Victor removed it and returned it to Van Dine.

"I think you're lying, Victor."

"I can explain."

"I'm sure you can. Sit down."

Victor sat as if his knees had given way.

Van Dine leaned forward, elbows on the table, fingers intertwined. "You are a very stupid man. And greedy; far too greedy for your own good. And for ours. Recently you robbed a group of *pollos* in the desert. Then you beat the man and left them all to die. Because of what you did, you brought us trouble and a great deal of attention that we didn't want."

"I took some money, yes," admitted Victor. "But the man attacked me."

"Why? For robbing him? Or did you also try to rape his wife? I think you did. You can't keep your hands out of other people's pockets. Or your *pinga* in your pants. *Estúpido,* Victor. *Estúpido.*"

Victor's head fell to his chest. "I apologize for everything I may have done. It won't happen again."

"You're right about that," Van Dine assured him. "It won't. As for forgiveness, maybe your 'priest' can forgive you. But I can't."

He nodded to Martinez and Placido. "Take him to the arroyo and shoot him."

Victor sprang from the chair. Martinez grabbed at his shoulder and missed. Victor bolted for the street. One foot was through the doorway, when the bullet from Placido's rifle caught him in the spine. Victor's body was flung forward, falling face down in the street.

"¡Vamos!" someone shouted from a truck.

Immediately the two trucks shot forward, their human cargo clinging to the railings, as the trucks accelerated down the street.

Van Dine, Martinez, and Placido watched them as they disappeared. Van Dine gestured toward the body in the street. "Both of you. Go to the arroyo, dig a grave, and bury him."

Van Dine looked across at Jon. "Dig two graves."

SEVENTEEN

VAN DINE WAITED until the two had taken Victor's body by the arms and dragged it away. Then he sat and leaned back in the chair. He spread his fingers out in front of him and cracked the knuckles at their joints. In the stillness of the room, it sounded like arms fire.

"Victor has been troublesome," Van Dine began. "But you've been a lot of trouble to us, also, Mr. Wilder. More than Victor, actually. I'll give you credit for inventiveness. Still, the real complication was putting yourself in Max Montoya's life. Or her putting herself in yours."

"It was you who told her to contact me," Jon reminded him.

"True, yes," Van Dine agreed. "She was presumably running the investigation. Unfortunately, she showed a tendency toward independence that was getting out of hand. Whatever information she learned wasn't supposed to go beyond a certain point. As her superior, she was required to report everything to me. It told me what she'd learned about us and enabled me to make adjustments in our operation if we had to. Even so, there was a detail I couldn't have foreseen," he said. "She fell in love with you."

"I don't think so."

"But she did. She fell in love with you and decided to involve you far more than was wise. I could have vetoed the idea at the start. I should have, but I thought your own ineptitude would only complicate her work. It turned out I was wrong."

"You knew I went to Terravita then?"

"Of course. After you spoke with her about your visit, she insisted on a stakeout. I couldn't let that happen."

"Did you kill Eric Voss?"

Van Dine was silent. He pulled a pack of cigarettes from his pocket, took one, and lit it. The match flared momentarily in the dark.

"Farolitos," Van Dine said, holding up the pack. "They're a Mexican brand. Martinez gave them to me when I ran out. Care for one?" He offered them to Jon.

"No."

"Just as well. They taste like rope." Van Dine returned the pack to his pocket and regarded Jon for several moments. "Concerning Eric Voss," he said at last, "he was careless when it came to using Terravita as a transfer point for illegals. I refused to send any of our *pollos* through there; I thought it was too dangerous. I even passed the word by way of an assistant that he should stop. He didn't, though. After you spotted the footprints in one of the Life Zones and in the pecan grove, I knew something needed to be done."

"The roadblock on the way to Tombstone was a setup, wasn't it?"

"I needed to be certain you and Max would be there," Van Dine said. He chuckled momentarily. "Of course, the reason I gave her for the roadblock was true. The Hawk *was* in the area. After you'd passed through, I discontinued it and sent Martinez on to Tombstone."

"Was he the shooter on the roof?"

"Marksmanship was never his strong point," Van Dine allowed.

"You could have killed the boy," Jon said.

"That wasn't my intention."

"Who was the target then? Max or me?"

"Either one of you," Van Dine said simply. "If she died, I was certain you'd give up your investigative efforts. If she lived, as I said, I'm her superior. I can determine what she knows and doesn't know."

Jon looked at him. "And she doesn't know you were the one who had her husband killed."

Once more, silence followed. "That was regrettable but necessary, I'm afraid," Van Dine said finally. "He suspected who the members of our operation were."

"Including you."

"Particularly me."

"What will happen to the investigation now?"

"It will die a quick and quiet death," Van Dine said. "Having been wounded in the line of duty, so to speak, Agent Montoya has been taken off the case. She may ask for reinstatement, but I don't believe she'll have the heart for it. Too many people she's loved will have died pursuing it. Tonight it will be you."

In the shadows of the room, the tip of Van Dine's cigarette glowed red. "As for what became of you," Van Dine went on, "all that is known is that you traveled into Mexico and disappeared, killed by *bandidos* or the drug gangs operating there. Naturally, no sign of a body will be found. And since you obviously entered Mexico under a false identity, no official record will exist that you were there."

"Let me ask you something," Jon said. "When we first met at the old mission, you told me you grew up in Minnesota."

Van Dine seemed puzzled. "Yes. My father was a Border Patrol agent at a place called Pigeon River. Why?"

"Because only someone who's lived east of the Rockies and heard the broad-winged hawk could imitate the call as well as you. When I listened to the sound Max's husband had recorded that night in Kyler's Pass, I wondered if you might somehow be involved."

"Indeed, I know the call quite well," Van Dine confirmed. "Every year, hundreds of broad-winged hawks migrate across Minnesota. As a boy, my father took me to a place called Hawk Ridge near Duluth to watch them passing over us. To me, they were the rulers of the skies. Once my father found a fledgling hawk that had been wounded by a hunter in the woods. My father and I nursed it: feeding it, tending to its wounds, until the bird was strong enough to fly. He trained the hawk to hunt and kill. He would release it into open country, and together we would watch as it killed smaller birds.'' Van Dine smiled. ''It was beautiful.''

''In Yuma,'' Jon said, ''you killed two Mexicans who worked as gardeners, didn't you? You stabbed them with their pruning shears, then scarred their bodies with a small hand rake. That's when they began calling you The Hawk. The victims looked as is they'd been mutilated by the talons of a bird. That must have given you some kind of ironic pleasure. The Hawk who killed the *pollos*.''

''Yes, I did.'' Again, a smile, thinner now. ''And yes. It gave me pleasure.''

Footsteps sounded from the boardwalk planks outside. Martinez entered, breathing heavily.

''Where's Placido?'' Van Dine demanded.

''He's having a hard time burying the body,'' Martinez said. ''There are rocks in the arroyo.''

''Is he still there?''

''Yes, sir.''

''What about the rifle?''

''Placido wanted to keep it.''

''And you let him?'' Van Dine was visibly annoyed. ''Get it. I want it.''

''Yes, sir.''

''Never mind.'' He waved a hand at Jon. ''I have a death for Mr. Wilder that's more appropriate than shooting him. Handcuff him.''

''Yes, sir.'' Martinez took a pair of handcuffs from his belt and cuffed Jon's hands behind his back.

''There's also rope in the car,'' Van Dine said. ''Get it.''

Martinez hurried from the building, once more puffing as he ran.

Van Dine drew a service revolver from a holster at his belt. "We're going for a nature walk," he said to Jon. "I know you enjoy taking people on such walks in order to observe the birds. Tonight you'll do the same for me. As soon as Martinez brings the rope, we'll go."

Van Dine leaned back in his chair and made an expansive gesture with his hands. "So, what do you think of our little town of Oro Rojo?"

"Charming."

"It was owned by Eric Voss. Did you know that? He talked about restoring it someday," Van Dine said. "In the meantime, he was good enough to let us use it as a transfer place for *pollos* now and then."

There was a wry look of amusement on his face. "But tonight the *pollos* have already flown, and after we complete our business, we, too, will fly into the night."

Martinez returned carrying a coil of rope and a lantern flashlight. "I'm here," he said, announcing what was obvious.

"We're going to the clearing." Van Dine took the lantern from Martinez's hand. "I'll lead the way."

Van Dine started across the room, focusing the lantern toward the street. From the jab Jon felt in his back, he knew Martinez had drawn his revolver, too. He followed Van Dine, with Martinez close behind.

They continued along the boardwalk to the corner of the building. Beyond it was an alleyway. Van Dine started down it, sweeping the lantern back and forth. From the darkness, a kangaroo rat scurried across their path. Martinez jumped and cursed at it in Spanish.

Behind the building the land rose among pines. From somewhere, the sound of a small stream could be heard. The path they climbed was wide and reasonably smooth, except for fallen pine needles that occasionally caused their feet to slip. Then, almost at once it became narrow and more primitive. Underfoot, Jon felt the gullies and sharp rocks that required them to slow their pace.

The trees and undergrowth were more difficult to penetrate. Branches seemed to fly out of the darkness at them as they walked. Behind him, Jon heard Martinez curse again as a branch of a piñon pine flew back in his face. Unable to use his hands to protect himself, Jon took to walking sideways up the slope with his head lowered. Twice his foot slipped on loose stones, causing him to slide into Martinez. Each time Martinez shoved the gun into his back.

At last, they found themselves in a small clearing, surrounded by Apache pines and canyon oaks. Van Dine made a slow sweep of the area, moving the beam of light from tree to tree. It came to rest on what had once been a tall pine. The tree appeared to have been struck by lightning. All that remained was a scarred and blackened trunk about ten feet in height, with broken stubs of branches near the top.

Van Dine waved the light in Jon's direction. "Take off his shirt and collar and tie him to the tree."

As Van Dine held the revolver and the lantern, Martinez dropped the rope on the ground, faced Jon, and ripped off the Roman collar. He tore open the shirt, then tried to yank down the sleeves.

"I can't get the shirt off while he's wearing handcuffs," Martinez said.

"Then leave the chest exposed. That's all I need."

Martinez did so, pulling open the shirt until Jon's chest was bare.

"Now tie him."

Martinez took the rope and pushed Jon back against the trunk of the pine. While Van Dine held the light on them, Martinez lashed Jon's legs to the trunk, then wound the rope several times around his upper chest under the arms. Jon felt sharp edges of the tree bark knifing into his back. He took a slow, deep breath to ease the pain. Martinez yanked the ends of the rope tight and stepped away.

"All right," Van Dine said. "That's enough. Get Placido and wait for me at the car. I'll be there soon."

"I can stay if—" Martinez started.

"Go," Van Dine insisted sharply. He swung the light into Martinez's face.

Martinez blinked, turned, and started back along the path, feeling his way in the dark.

In the silence of the woods, there was no sound except the whisper of a breeze that had begun to stir. Jon felt it on his chest and shivered. His chest was bathed in sweat.

"So—" Van Dine said, redirecting the light toward him. "This is the kind of place where you'd conduct a nature walk. Am I correct?"

"Yes."

"I've also heard that as an ornithologist, you're very popular. With your experience and knowledge, you're able to tell what birds are native to this area, even without seeing them. That's quite an accomplishment."

Jon said nothing.

"But now, it's just the two of us," Van Dine went on. "I consider myself honored, Mr. Wilder, to be your audience of one. The last person to hear you lecture on the birds the night you died. Tell me—what birds would we have around us in the woods? If it was daylight, what birds would I see?"

"Woodpeckers. Quail."

"Specifics," Van Dine urged. "What kind of woodpeckers and quail?"

"The acorn woodpecker. The Montezuma quail."

"Very good. You obviously know your birds." Van Dine was taking pleasure in the ridicule.

"Continue. There must be others," Van Dine said. "Tell me what they are."

"Because we passed a stream," Jon said, "there could be yellow warblers, and—"

Jon stopped. In the branches of the oak above where Van Dine stood, something moved. For a brief instant, Jon could see its head. It gave him an idea.

"That's enough," Van Dine said suddenly. "It's late." He seemed to be tiring of the game. Holstering the gun, he drew a small hand rake from inside his jacket. In the light, the three curved metal points gleamed.

"Before you use that," Jon said, "I should tell you that we're being watched."

"Really? Are we?"

Awakened by the voices, the thing rose up among the branches of the tree. It shook its head, opening its sharp, curving beak, then spread its wide red tail like a fan.

"And where is this so-called watcher?" Van Dine asked.

"In the tree above you."

The beam of Van Dine's lantern shot up.

"Keeeer-rr!" The cry burst from Jon's throat, a high-pitched wail shattering the night.

Alarmed, the huge red-tailed hawk extended its wings, dislodging sticks and twigs that rained down on Van Dine.

Dropping the hand rake, Van Dine seized his revolver and began firing wildly into the branches of the tree.

Wings spread, the panicked hawk began to fly. A bullet caught it in the side: The bird shrieked, flapped its wings, and fell straight down onto Van Dine's upturned face.

"No! Stop! My face!"

Now it was Van Dine screaming, falling backward. The talons of the wounded hawk continued tearing at his face.

Jon turned away.

Van Dine's screams had become agonizing moans. The hawk could be heard, also, its quick, shrill cries of pain combining with the futile beating of its wings.

When Jon looked again, the hawk was managing to rise. Suddenly it dropped and rolled on its side, one wing upraised, but alive.

Then, gradually, Jon heard another sound: people moving through the woods. Lights showed through the trees below him, growing brighter, closer.

"Jon—are you there?" someone called out. "Jon?" It was Max Montoya's voice.

EIGHTEEN

THE RINGING OF the telephone cut through Jon's sub-
conscious, waking him after a few hours of exhausted
sleep.

The caller was Agent Somebody-or-Other from
Border Patrol headquarters in Tucson requesting that
he appear at four o'clock that afternoon. A car would
be waiting at the front entrance of the Wolfshead Inn
at three. The caller hung up before Jon could speak.

After arriving at the headquarters building before
four, Jon was led to what appeared to be an interrogation room and asked to wait. He waited for an hour,
seated in a metal chair that faced a table and two other
chairs. The walls were gray. The single window was
encased in sturdy wire mesh. There was no piano
stool. Otherwise, *La Boca*'s office was beginning to
seem friendly in comparison.

At five-fifteen, the door of the room opened. One
man entered, followed by a second man. Both were in
their forties. Dressed in dark suits, white shirts, and
dark ties, they had the bearing of morticians at a particularly boring funeral. The second man wore rimless
glasses and carried an attaché case. He closed the door
behind him, locking it.

"Mr. Webster?" the first man said.

"Wilder."

He shook Jon's hand perfunctorily, as did the second man. Both sat opposite him on the far side of the table.

"I'm Ed Nachman from the INS," the first man went on. He gestured toward the second man. "This is Walter Benedict from Justice. Excuse the time. Our plane from Washington was late."

The second man nodded in concurrence but said nothing.

"Thank you for agreeing to talk with us," Nachman said.

He reached into an inner pocket of his jacket and withdrew some notes. He consulted them for several moments. Then he looked at Jon. "From what we understand, you had something of an unpleasant ordeal last night."

"Oro Rojo isn't on my list of recommended tourist spots," Jon said.

Neither of the men seemed to catch the irony.

"Can you tell us what occurred?" Nachman asked.

"I've already given a full statement to the Border Patrol and the police."

"I know. But we'd like to hear it for ourselves."

"Van Dine and Martinez took me up into the clearing," Jon said. "Martinez tied me to a tree. After he left, Van Dine was about to kill me, when I noticed something in the tree above where Van Dine stood. It was a large red-tailed hawk. When I told Van Dine we were being watched, he shined the light into the tree. It spooked the bird. I made the hawk's cry of alarm and the bird started to fly. Not knowing what it was, Van Dine shot at it and wounded it. The hawk fell directly down on him and began clawing at his face.''

"That's when Agent Montoya and the others arrived?''

"Yes. The sheriff's officers were there soon after that. It was past dawn when they finally got me back to the inn.''

The two men exchanged glances. Nothing in their expressions suggested whether they believed him or not.

Nachman turned to Jon again. He seemed to be choosing his words carefully. "To be candid, what occurred last night was something of an embarrassment for all of us.''

"An *embarrassment?*''

Nachman held his hands in front of him, placing his fingertips together in a reflective, almost prayerful gesture. "Let me explain something. Hear me out. Some good can come of all of this. Or it cannot. It all depends on you.''

"What are you trying to tell me?'' Jon asked.

"That we need your understanding and cooperation.''

"How?''

"To begin with, we agree that Van Dine and Martinez were bad apples,'' Nachman said. "But in fact, the majority of Border Patrol agents are dedicated law enforcement officers. And we need more of them.

Next month, the Immigration and Naturalization Service is inaugurating a promotional campaign to recruit more men and women to the force. If it became known that Agent Van Dine was the leader of a criminal smuggling operation, it could be detrimental to those efforts. Also, Mexico has a new president, as do we. In the spirit of mutual cooperation between countries, we wish to avoid anything that could be diplomatically disadvantageous to both.''

"What you're suggesting," Jon said bluntly, "is that you don't want any of this known."

"Correct."

"It'll become known when Van Dine goes to trial."

Nachman cleared his throat. "It may not come to that."

"What do you mean, 'it may not come to that'?"

"Agent Van Dine provided many years of conscientious service before he chose—how shall I put it?—another path. This morning he offered to disclose the names of both Americans and Mexicans who are currently involved in smuggling activities. In exchange, we're prepared to seek a reduction in whatever sentence he receives."

"The man's a killer and a sadist," Jon insisted.

"Remember, also," Nachman said, "Van Dine's face was terribly disfigured by the talons of the bird. He will be permanently blind. I call that justice of a sort."

"And I call it a cop-out," Jon shot back. "Do you know how many people died because of him? Or were they also 'embarrassments' you'd just as soon forget?

If Agent Montoya and the others hadn't shown up, I could still be tied to a tree in Oro Rojo.''

Again, the two men across the table shared a look.

Nachman pursed his lips. "Frankly, as successful as her efforts were, Agent Montoya exceeded her authority in coming to your aid without approval from superiors.''

"Van Dine was her superior! Was she supposed to ask *him?*''

"There were others,'' Nachman said. "Procedures that she should have followed.''

"And before anybody would have acted on them, I'd be dead.'' Jon took a breath. "Look—I'm very tired. So before I say something I regret, I suggest we end this and you find a driver who can take me back to Wolfshead now.''

"We'll do that,'' Nachman told him. "After you've signed the statement we've prepared.''

"What statement?''

"A statement of confidentiality.''

"About what?''

"What we've discussed.''

"And if I don't?'' Jon asked.

"You could be indicted on a variety of charges,'' Nachman told him, leaning forward as he spoke. "Obtaining a forged passport. Entering Mexico illegally. The obstruction of a federal investigation.''

Nachman paused. "We also know who furnished you the fraudulent visa.'' He consulted his notes. "I believe his name is…Father Francis Flannery of St. Anne's Church in Santa Rita.''

"So if I sign this document, I'm saying none of these things happened."

Nachman stared at him in silence. Benedict opened the attaché case and removed a sheet of paper. He slid it across the table to Jon.

"That's right," Nachman said. "None of these things happened."

He offered Jon a pen.

THE SOUND WAS FAINT: the low murmur of the engine as a vehicle moved over the desert sand.

Jon turned and shaded his eyes against the sun. The markings of the Border Patrol car were visible. It came to a stop near the old mission. Max stepped out. She was dressed in her green uniform.

"I found your message when I got back to the office," she said. "I was on patrol when you called."

"I was afraid I missed you," Jon said.

"You mentioned you were stopping by the mission. I took a chance you'd still be here."

"I'm glad you did."

"Why did you come?" she asked. "I'm curious. Revisiting the place where all of this began?"

"That's part of it," Jon told her. "Today is also Angélica's birthday. Emilio wanted to bring flowers here, but it was very hard for him. I said I'd bring them in his place."

"That was nice of you."

"Emilio is a good friend."

"Your message also said that you'd be leaving," she continued. "When?"

"This afternoon. I have some old friends in Sedona. We spoke last night, and they invited me to stay with them for a few days."

"Sedona is a lovely town." Max paused. "By the way, I heard about your meeting yesterday. The one with Nachman and the other fed."

"He was the one who drew up the statement of confidentiality," Jon said. "It read like something a Justice Department lawyer would draft."

"Did you sign it?"

"No."

Max smiled. "Good for you."

"Or not. I'll probably be indicted."

"No, you won't," she said. "I checked. The two of them—Nachman, in particular—were supporters of Van Dine. When Van Dine's plans for Operation Sandstorm were reviewed and questioned by others at the INS, Nachman went to his defense. And so did Benedict. Now both are trying to save their asses and their jobs by making it seem like none of this occurred."

"Nachman said they'd seek a reduced sentence for Van Dine."

Max shook her head. "They went to court and tried. I'm glad to say the prosecutor and the judge thought otherwise. Van Dine is facing twenty-five to life, no matter what."

"Nachman was right about one thing," Jon said. "That hawk delivered its own kind of justice on Van Dine."

"It's still not enough to make up for all the misery and death he caused."

"You never told me how you tracked me down in Oro Rojo," Jon said.

"The day after I saw you in the hospital, I tried to call you at the inn. They said you were no longer there. I phoned Emilio and asked him where you'd gone. In the beginning, he was vague. But when I pressed him, he admitted what you'd done. He also said he'd dropped you off in San Miguel. So I contacted one of our informants there."

"You have an informant in San Miguel?" Jon asked.

"Gustavo. He's the bartender-cook at the cantina."

"I hope his information is better than his eggs."

"Gustavo told me you were on a bus with *pollos* who would be smuggled into the U.S. that night. From another source, we also heard that the *coyotes* planned a stop at Oro Rojo and that *El Halcón* might be there. So I checked myself out of the hospital and went to work. The trouble was, I had to arrange the operation without Van Dine knowing anything about it. That's the reason we were later than we hoped in getting to you."

"What made you suspect Van Dine to begin with?"

"After Roberto died, Van Dine kept asking if my husband had information on the smugglers he should know about. I lied and told him no. And that roadblock on the way to Tombstone made no sense. Van Dine set it up the night before and assigned himself and Martinez to be part of it. That way he'd be certain I would be in Tombstone as I'd said. But what confirmed Van Dine's involvement were the carpet fibers found in Voss's wounds.''

"You mentioned that a friend in the medical examiner's office was running tests to see if they matched those on the jackrabbit.''

"Yes. But after the report had passed through Van Dine's hands, there was no mention of the fibers anywhere,'' Max said. "I thought the tests might have come up empty. So I called the M.E.''s office and spoke with my friend.''

"And?''

"He said, on the contrary, the tests showed evidence in both cases that the fibers came from the floor carpeting Ford uses in their Expedition vehicles. Somehow, Van Dine had deleted any reference to it in the report. After more checking, I'm sure they'll find it was the Expedition that Van Dine was driving on the nights the jackrabbit and Eric Voss were killed.''

"What about Martinez and the boy?'' Jon asked.

"We found them waiting in a vehicle parked on a side street in Oro Rojo.''

"Was it a white Chevy Blazer with a broken headlight, by any chance?''

"How did you know?''

"It followed me the day of the flash flood.''

"We learned it belonged to Martinez,'' Max confirmed.

"The boy must have driven it that day,'' Jon said. "After he passed me on the interstate, he probably headed to the Wolfshead road to set up the false detour.''

"Well, now, at least, The Hawk and all his evil little fledglings are in custody or dead, like Victor,'' she assured him.

"For a while I thought Billy Ketchum might be involved, too. Particularly after running into him in Tombstone.''

"Ketchum is too dumb to have masterminded anything like this.'' Max paused. "But just between us, I'm convinced we'll get him soon on other charges. Yesterday he hired a Mexican illegal as a housekeeper. That is, he thinks she's an illegal. The fact is she's an undercover agent. Billy Ketchum's days as an equal opportunity employer are over.''

"I'm glad to hear it,'' Jon said.

An awkward silence fell between them. Max brushed back a wisp of hair and turned away. As she did, Jon saw her eyes were wet.

Turning back to him, she asked, "So are you driving directly to Sedona after you leave here? I mean, not stopping in Tucson—or someplace?''

"No,'' Jon said. "But if I hadn't heard from you, I'd planned to visit sector headquarters and leave a note for you.''

"This is better.'' Max managed a wistful smile. "Now, while I'm driving west today, I'll think about you driving north.''

"Where are you going?''

"Yuma,'' Max said.

"Is it part of an assignment?''

"No." She shook her head. "The Yuma station offered me a transfer to their sector. They want to talk to me this afternoon."

"Will you accept it?"

"I already have. Tom said he's looking for a place for Bobito and me. Bobito's excited. He likes Tom a lot."

"And you?"

"Tom's been a good friend since Roberto died."

"When will you be moving?"

"In a few weeks, I hope. Soon enough for Bobito to start school."

"I'm glad for you," Jon said. "Tom seems like a good man."

Max reached down and took his hand. "He is. But so are you. Except for Roberto, you have more courage than any man I've ever met. I'll always think of you as *El Águila*—the eagle. Like the eagle on the Mexican flag destroying the snake, your courage brought a lot of snakes to justice."

"Maybe it would have been better if I'd been an owl," Jon admitted. "Wise and cautious. Several times I blundered into situations where you had to save my life. That took some courage, too."

Max smiled. "Saving lives is part of what we do, whether it's *pollos* stranded in the desert or people who take on bad guys like Van Dine and end up being tied, half naked, to a tree."

"Anyway—thank you."

"De nada," she replied.

They looked at one another. Neither spoke. Finally

Max checked her watch. "It's time for me to go," she said.

"I should be going, too."

"Well...good-bye."

Now Jon took both her hands in his and pulled her close to him. She put her head against his chest.

"*Te quiero,* Jon," she told him in a whisper.

Stroking her face, he discovered there were tears. "*Te quiero también,*" he said. "I love you, too."

"I know." She ran a hand across her face, then turned and walked away. Moments later, she was gone.

Jon watched as the Border Patrol vehicle disappeared against the sun. Then he, too, started for his car.

HIGH ABOVE, the solitary creature glided, its wings buoyed by the thermal currents rising from the desert floor. Circling, the bird observed the figure far below. The bird's senses were remarkably acute, its tiny black eyes able to spot prey as small as desert mice from several hundred feet.

What it saw now, however, was of no interest to the bird. It was in search of carrion. Rarely did it attack living things, and then only if the prey was small and weak, or it was sure that death would follow soon.

Had the bird more than a dim, elemental memory, it would remember other figures such as this one moving slowly over the same sands. One by one they had lain down and become still. At the time, the bird was briefly curious. But seeing other birds descending on the carcass of a coyote pup not far away, it had flown off to join them.

Hours afterward, when it returned to this place, it had smelled the smell of death. But this time there were many figures moving swiftly and great objects making loud, harsh noises that drove the bird away.

When it returned again at dusk, all was as it was before. The many figures and the great objects were gone, and the bird saw only the ruined stones of the old mission.

Yet this, at least, it knew.

In the days to come, other figures would appear as those had many days before. In the end, they, too, would lie down on the sand and die.

And high above the bird would watch for them.

And wait.

SKELETONS
IN PURPLE SAGE

BARBARA BURNETT SMITH

A JOLIE WYATT MYSTERY

A flash flood in the town of Purple Sage leaves a local doctor dead. The police are calling it an accident, but amateur sleuth Jolie Wyatt suspects murder.

The doctor died on the night he was an honored guest at a reception for the Texas governor and when Jolie stumbles upon the body of the unpopular hostess she confirms that something sinister is going on.

Like the receding flood waters, the truth reveals a nasty mess, especially as Jolie wades through the muck to the identity of a killer waiting to send Jolie to her grave.

"...appealing..."
—Booklist

Available January 2004.

 WORLDWIDE LIBRARY ®

WBS479